Lauren,
Hide God's Word
in your heart !

THE ADVENTURES

OF MATTHEW AND ANDY
GENESIS

STEVE E. UPCHURCH

WESTBOW
PRESS®
A DIVISION OF THOMAS NELSON
& ZONDERVAN

WestBow Press books may be ordered through booksellers or by contacting:

WestBow Press
A Division of Thomas Nelson & Zondervan
1663 Liberty Drive
Bloomington, IN 47403
www.westbowpress.com
1 (866) 928-1240

ISBN: 978-1-5127-0943-8 (sc)
ISBN: 978-1-5127-0944-5 (hc)
ISBN: 978-1-5127-0942-1 (e)

Library of Congress Control Number: 2015914007

Print information available on the last page.

WestBow Press rev. date: 09/24/2015

Matthew is a ten year old boy who has started reading his Bible. However, he struggles trying to understand the Bible stories. One night in his dreams a short, chubby angel shows up and starts taking Matthew back in time to see firsthand how each story unfolds. Matthew tells us in vivid detail what he sees in the Bible from the viewpoint of a fifth grade boy.

CONTENTS

INTRODUCTION

My name is Matthew. My name comes from the Bible. Matthew is the name of the first book in the New Testament. And since I am the first child that was born to my mom and dad, they named me Matthew. I like being named after someone in the Bible. But I'm glad they didn't go for a long name … like Nebuchadnezzar!!!

My dad says that names in the Bible have meaning. And he said that my name is one of the oldest names and it means "*gift from God*." When he told me that, it made me smile. I am a gift from God!

I am ten years old, and in the fifth grade. A few days ago, Carl Johnson, the class bully, the meanest kid in my class, started making fun of me. He started calling me a "Bible thumper." Some of the other kids also started laughing at me. I didn't know what a "Bible thumper" was, but Mom said it's a name that has been used for a long time to make fun of someone that believes the Bible. But then she told me that I should be proud, because some snooty people in the Bible also made fun of Matthew. She said he collected taxes before he met Jesus, and in those days being a tax collector was not a very popular job.

Mom also said that even though some people didn't like Matthew, the tax collector, look how it turned out for him. She said that millions of people over the past two thousand years know who Matthew the tax collector was! But more importantly, she said people know what he ended up being … one of the disciples of Jesus!

Who knows, maybe someday I'll be famous too!

Mom gave me some very good advice. She said that if anyone calls me a "Bible thumper" anymore, I should think of Thumper the rabbit in the story about Bambi.

And guess what? I tried it and it worked! The very next day Carl called me a" Bible thumper" again, and I said, "Yes I am!" And I started thumping my foot on the ground and jumping around like Thumper did in the movie. And all the kids started laughing. But this time they weren't laughing at me, instead, they were all laughing with me.

And Jenny, one of the fourth grade girls, told me she thought I was cool! And EVERYBODY likes Jenny!

So now not only has Carl stopped making fun of me, he is actually being nice to me. And … it seems like Jenny really likes me.

✳ ✳ ✳ ✳

Now, let me tell you about someone named Andy. Andy is an angel. He is my angel.

I remember once Pastor Mark, was talking about how each person has their very own angel. On the way home from church that day, Dad and Mom were talking about what Pastor Mark said. Dad said he thought Pastor Mark was exaggerating. He said that if each person had their own angel, then there would have to be millions of angels. Mom said she agreed with Pastor Mark. She said she was pretty sure she had read something about it in the Bible.

I really wanted to know for sure, so I asked Mom if we could look it up when we got home. So when we got home, Mom got out her laptop computer, and we googled what the Bible says about angels.

And guess what? It's true!

Mom read from Psalm chapter 91, verses 11 and 12, where it says that God not only has given His angels instructions to watch over us in all that we do, but they watch out for us so that we don't dash our foot against a stone, meaning God watches out for us and protects us from things that may harm us.

And then she found a verse in the book of Matthew (yes the guy in the Bible I am named after) chapter 18, and verse 10 that says that the angels of children always see the face of God in heaven! Each child has their own special angel that watches over them. How cool is that?

I was really glad to find out that it's okay that I do have my own personal angel, because Andy had been showing up in my dreams for quite a while. It was good to find out I wasn't coo-coo!

I finally got up enough nerve to tell Mom about Andy. I told her that since he shows up here on earth in my dreams, I call him my "earth angel." When I said that she started laughing, so I asked her what was so funny. She said there is an old song about an earth angel. Hmmm... I don't get it.

But Andy is the coolest angel ever. He is not like any of the pictures of angels in Grandma's big family Bible. All of those angels are tall and look very beautiful, with long flowing wings.

Not Andy!!!

Andy is short, like me. And he has bright red curly hair and lots of freckles on his face. He's also a little bit chubby, with skinny legs. And his wings ... well ... they are not long and flowing like the other angel's wings. His wings are short. He actually reminds me of an ostrich, with his short little wings and his skinny legs.

And instead of wearing a long white robe, like the angels in Grandma's big family Bible, Andy wears a basketball jersey with the number "23" on it. He also has on short baggy shorts, that do not cover his skinny legs, and he always has on tennis shoes.

He likes to imitate Michael Jordon jumping high through the air!!!

Andy's not mean, but after I told mom some of the things he does and says, she said it sounds like he has an ornery streak in him. I told her I didn't know that that meant. She said that means a person is good on the inside, but sometimes they get in trouble on the outside! And I do know what that is like. That is what Mrs. Underwood, my fifth grade teacher, says is wrong with me!

One day Mrs. Underwood gave me a time out for talking in class. She told me that I had to sit in the corner. When she saw me sitting there smiling she asked what I was up to. I told her, "I may be sitting down on the *outside*, but I'm playing basketball on the *inside*!"

The first time I met Andy was shortly after I started reading my Bible every day. I really wanted to read my Bible every day, like Pastor Mark said we should do, but sometimes I had a hard time understanding what it meant.

Then Andy started showing up in my dreams.

Andy has a very special talent. *He can go back in time!* And in my dreams he takes me with him. I just climb on his back, the same way I climb on my dad's back when he acts like he is a horse!

I'm sure we look funny ... a short, blond headed fifth grade boy riding on the back of a short, chubby, red headed angel, with short little wings that flutter real fast!

Yes, I am positive that we look funny. But that's okay. I sure am learning a lot about the Bible!

CHAPTER 1: THE CREATION ADVENTURE

I heard, "Climb aboard!"

Andy the angel said, "Let's go see how the earth was made."

In my dream I jumped on his back. His wings began to flutter so fast it reminded me of a humming bird. And off we went!

I don't mind telling you that for the first several minutes it was pretty scary. I don't know who gave Andy his license to fly, but God really needs to find out who it was and have a serious talk with him!

Have you ever played the game where you stand a baseball bat up on its end, place your head on the top of the bat, spin in circles ten times, and then try to run to first base? You try your best to run in a straight line, but it's like there's a giant magnet that pulls you sideways.

That is what it was like flying with Andy! First we went one way, and then the other. And on top of his crazy flying skills, the tips of his wing kept brushing against my nose, which made me start sneezing.

And every time I sneezed, we would go straight up in the air! So we were going back and forth from side to side, and we were also going up and down! I felt like I was riding a roller coaster!

Finally Andy got things under control. Thank goodness, because I was getting ready to throw up.

Once he sensed I was okay he asked me, "What did you read in your Bible last night?"

I said, "I started reading in the beginning, in the first chapter of Genesis."

"Great!" Andy exclaimed. "That is where we will start our first adventure."

So off we flew to see creation day.

The farther we flew, the darker it became... until we reached utter and complete darkness. It was so dark I could not see my hand in front of my face.

And it was cold! Bitter cold. The kind of cold that sinks into your skin and makes your bones hurt.

I was getting scared, so I leaned forward and whispered loudly in Andy's ear, "Why is it so dark and cold?"

He replied, "Didn't you read the first chapter of Genesis before you went to bed last night?"

"Yes."

"Then you should remember how it said that in the beginning, God had created the heavens and the earth. And how, at first the earth had no form... and was covered in darkness. If it was dark, that meant there was no sun. And if there was no sun, there was no heat."

"Okay. Now I understand. But I wish you had warned me so I could have brought a coat!"

"Hey Matthew ..."

"Yes."

"You do realize this is a dream don't you?"

"Yes ..."

"Then you are dreaming that you are cold!"

That helped a little bit. But the farther we flew, the darker it became - until I couldn't even see Andy right there beneath me!

And I sure was glad I had Andy's feathers all around me because I know I would have frozen, dream or not!

As we flew into the darkness, I remembered the story my grandpa told me about how he worked deep below the surface of the earth in the coal mines.

He said he would take an elevator down a deep dark hole in the ground for several hundred feet. And then he would get off the elevator and walk long distances in underground tunnels to go to where he loaded coal cars.

He said that sometimes he would take a nap during his lunch break. When he did he said he would turn off the electric lights that were in the tunnels, and he would also turn off the light that was on his helmet.

I remember how he described the darkness. He said it was "penetrating darkness ... a darkness so thick and heavy you could almost feel it."

✷ ✷ ✷ ✷

And now in my dream, I could feel that kind of darkness. I was completely surrounded by the overwhelming feeling of nothingness.

It was hard to breathe.

There wasn't even the slightest breeze.

Everything around us felt dead.

There was no life.

The place where Andy had taken me was just like Genesis chapter 1, verse 2. It was void of everything! And darkness was on the face of the deep!

Have you ever been in a deep sleep and suddenly you knew your mom was there by your bed watching you?

There in the darkness I had that same feeling. There in that mind-numbing darkness I suddenly felt that we were in the presence of *someone*. I could sense that we were in the presence of a great and powerful spiritual being!

At first I felt completely terrified. And then Andy reached over in the darkness and put his hand on my shoulder and whispered, "It's going to be okay. But you might want to put these on and make sure you keep your eyes open. You are going to want to see this!"

Then Andy placed something in my hand.

"What is this?" I whispered.

"A pair of sunglasses," he replied.

"Are you crazy?" I asked. "Why do I need sunglasses when all around us is nothing but complete darkness?"

"Just wait ... you'll see!" he whispered.

Then out of the darkness, the "presence" suddenly spoke!

Last week in class, our teacher, Mrs. Underwood, was not in a good mood. And she warned the whole class that during "quiet time" she did not want to hear one peep out of us.

I was doing just fine until she said that! But as soon as she warned us to be quiet, for some reason all I could think of was - how my nose was starting to itch.

And then the itch turned into a tickle.

And then the tickle turned into a sneeze.

Have you ever tried to hold in a sneeze? It's like blowing up a tiny balloon. It gets bigger … and bigger … and bigger. And then … boom! *It explodes!*

That was how my sneeze was - my breath came gushing out of my mouth and my nose!

There was spit and snot everywhere!

And because it happened during "quiet time," it sounded even louder!

★ ★ ★ ★

That's what it felt like in my dream when the Creator finally spoke.

Everything was eerily quiet … and then suddenly there was this loud, deep, booming voice.

"Let there be light!"

It's hard to believe that creation began with those four, little words.

And no sooner had God spoke when suddenly out of the darkness came an explosion!

It was like there were thousands of flashes of lightning and thousands of clashes of thunder all going off at the same time!

God had just created the sun!

Even with those sunglasses on, I was temporarily blinded by the cascade of brilliant light that flooded the earth where Andy and I were standing.

And even though the suns explosion took place over sixty three million miles away where we stood on the earth, the force of the blast picked me up and threw me to the ground!

What just happened?" I asked as I tried to gather my senses. My head felt like the recess bell was going off inside my head! My ears were ringing and my eyes were watering.

Andy replied, "You have just witnessed the biggest firecracker explosion that will ever be recorded in history!"

Cool," I said in amazement as I scrambled back to my feet. Then it dawned on me that I had witnessed just a small glimpse of the awesome power of almighty God!

With the speaking of those four little words, "let there be light," the entire universe would now be visible for all to see. Millions of stars and the moon would now reflect the light from the sun.

The earth where we were standing would now receive light and heat. It suddenly dawned on me just how perfect God's creation had been. If the earth had been placed just slightly closer to the sun, all of the ice at the North Pole would melt away and the heat would be unbearable. And if the sun was just slightly farther away, the whole earth would be completely covered with ice.

It was just like the bowl of soup in the story about the three bears. *Not too hot … not too cold … but just right!*

Andy could tell I was deep in thought. "Let me show you something to help you understand what you just witnessed," he said.

From his bag he took out a basketball and a small marble.

"This basketball represents the size of the sun, and this little marble is the size of the earth. The sun is 109 times bigger than the earth."

"Wow! I didn't realize just how big the sun was!" I exclaimed.

"Guess what I have done?" asked Andy. "I filled this basketball with gasoline. But I have to give you the strictest of warnings, and that is that you never, ever, try this at home, because gasoline is very explosive! Now stand way over there. I'm going to set this basketball on fire!"

"Whoa… are you sure this is going to be okay? My dad threatened me with the worst spanking ever if he ever caught me playing with gasoline and matches!"

"Don't worry," Andy said. "You just stand way over there while I set it on fire. And cover your ears because there is going to be a major explosion."

Andy lit the ball with a match and then turned and flew toward me as fast as his little ostrich wings could flutter!

"Boom!"

The ground shook as flaming pieces of the basketball flew past us!

"Now, has anyone tried to tell you that everything we see on earth is the result of a Big Bang?" asked Andy.

"Yes. Mr. Lou, our science teacher, told us that a few weeks ago. He said that everything started millions of years ago with a Big Bang."

"Well, he may be partly right" responded Andy. "As you just witnessed, when God ignited that huge ball of hydrogen we know as the sun, the bang that happened was the biggest bang ever experienced in history. However, they are completely wrong with the results of their theory."

"What happened to the ball that we just blew up?" Andy asked.

I walked around and picked up some of the pieces of the exploded ball. "There is absolutely nothing left except for these burnt pieces lying around" I said.

"Exactly" replied Andy. "An explosion of that magnitude would only create destruction and chaos. Their theory is the Big Bang explosion resulted in the exact opposite of what we just witnessed. They think the Big Bang explosion resulted in trillions of life forms being created."

"That makes absolutely no sense to me now!" I answered. "An explosion that big would *destroy* everything, not *create* everything!"

"Good! You are now smarter than a lot of college professors!" Andy said. "Now, climb aboard, it's time to go back home."

Fortunately the ride back home was not quite as bumpy as the first ride. Andy was starting to get the hang of flying with me riding on his back.

The next thing I knew, we were in the parking lot at my grade school.

"What are we doing here?" I asked.

"We are going to perform one more experiment."

"Okay."

"Do you know how these rocks in the parking lot were made?"

"No."

"Huge bulldozers uncovered layers of rock found in the earth. Then dynamite was used to blow the solid rock into pieces that could to be loaded and moved. Then those large pieces of rock were run through a rock crusher to make them the size that you see now. So basically all of these rocks were created by a *big bang*, right?"

"It sure sounds like it."

"Now I want you to walk around the parking lot and randomly pick up fifty rocks and bring them inside to the science lab."

I did just what Andy asked. I held out the bottom of my t-shirt, picked up fifty rocks and placed them inside and took them into the science lab and placed them on a table.

"Now," Andy said, "I want you to go through these fifty rocks and pick out five of the rocks that look the most like a ball."

"You want me to find the five rocks that are the most shaped like a ball?"

"Yep! Pick out the five that you think are the most round."

After ten minutes and careful inspection I had my five selections.

While I was selecting the rocks, Andy had opened a science book to the page that showed actual photographs of the sun, the earth, Mars, Venus, Jupiter and several other planets.

"Let's look at your five rock selections," Andy said.

"What are we looking for?"

"Do you see these actual pictures of the planets surrounding the earth?"

"Yes."

"What shape does each one of them have?"

"They are all perfectly round, like a ball."

"Now look at the rocks you selected. Do any of them have the perfect shape of a ball like the photographs of these planets?"

"No! None of them have that perfect shape!" I exclaimed.

I was really excited. I was starting to get it. The Big Bang Theory could not possibly be right. There is no way an explosion could result in every planet that surrounds us ending up being perfectly round!

Then Andy reached into his bag and pulled out a golf ball.

"Check out this ball closely, and tell me what you see."

I held the ball close to my eyes and looked it over carefully.

"I see little bumps."

"Those are called dimples."

"What else do you see?"

"I see the word *Titleist*."

"And what does that tell you?"

"That this ball was created by someone for a specific purpose?"

"Correct."

Then another light bulb went off in my head.

"I get it! I get it! I get it!" I shouted.

"The dimples on the golf ball are like the mountains and valleys of earth. But from a distance it looks perfectly round!"

"What about the name on the ball?" asked Andy.

"The name on the ball tells us who made it!"

Andy smiled. His mission for tonight was completed. Then he floated away.

I woke up and lay there in my bed thinking about my first adventure with Andy. I turned on my side and looked out my bedroom window. There shining into my bedroom was the brightness of a full moon.

And then I felt it.

It was the same *presence* that was in my dream. The same Creator that said "Let there be light", was now right there in my bedroom with me. But instead of feeling terrified like I did when I first felt the presence of God, now I felt very calm and peaceful!

As I drifted back off to sleep I know it was my imagination but I was sure I saw three words printed there on the moon.

Made By God.

And just like Andy smiled as he floated away, I smiled as I floated back to sleep.

Discuss the following questions with your parents or a friend:

- Does a "Big Bang" create things or destroy things?
- What happened to the gas filled ball when it made a big bang?
- How many ball-shaped rocks did they find in the parking lot?
- To what was the golf ball compared?

CHAPTER 2: YOU LOOK JUST LIKE YOUR FATHER

Did you brush your teeth?"

"Yes mom!"

"Did you wash behind your ears?"

"Yes mom!"

I didn't say it, but I thought it... *Who looks behind a person's ear unless they are looking for a magician's hidden quarter?*

"Did you comb your hair?"

"Yes mom!"

"Did you put on the clothes I laid out for you?"

"Yes mom!"

Why are these questions reserved only for boys? I have never once heard my mom ask my little sister, "Did you put on clean underwear today?"

But for me, it's a daily occurrence.

And today is especially bad. We are getting our annual family photos taken, which means I have to put on a stupid fake smile.

Stand up straight... "*Tip your head slightly to the right. Now hold it. Don't move. Say "cheese"!*

Geesh! The only cheese I was thinking about was a *cheese-burger*!

11

And then we usually have to do it all over again because mom didn't think that one little strand of her hair was quite in the right position.

I could also see that this was going to be one of those "yes, dear" days for my dad.

Let me make this clear. There is nothing my dad can't do. He works on the house. He works on the car. He can fix almost anything.

And he is tough! I once saw him scare off the meanest looking stray pit bull dog I had ever seen that wandered into our yard.

Not only that, he has a box of medals that he received for bravery when he fought in the war in Iraq.

So my dad is one bad dude!

But for some reason on days like today my tough dad becomes a zombie that only knows how to mumble two words. *"Yes dear."*

And mom has a whole separate list of questions for my dad. Which lets me know that on days like today it doesn't matter how old you are… if you are a male the day will go much better if you simply learn to respond with *"Yes, dear"*.

What is it about a camera that causes people to change how they would normally act? It even affects grandpa. He can be as calm and quiet as can be, but if someone points a camera at him he takes on a whole different personality. He goes from sitting there like a piece of furniture, to being the class clown. He starts making faces and trying to hold *rabbit ears* behind my head with two fingers!

Hmmm… maybe that is where I get my orneriness!

Anyway, we spent the afternoon getting our pictures taken. And as a result of me and dad "being good boys," mom said we could stop and get some ice cream.

At first I thought that mom calling dad a "boy" was a bit of a stretch. But after watching him eat his ice cream cone I think I understood.

By the time it was over he had ice cream on his shirt, on his tie, in his lap! He even got some on his shoes and socks. How did he get ice cream on his socks?

Hmmm… maybe that is where I get that as well!

That night before I went to sleep I read in my Bible how God created Adam and Eve. With thoughts of getting my picture taken, I drifted off to sleep.

Then Andy showed up!

Ready for another adventure up onto his back I jumped and away we went.

"Hey Andy!" I shouted, "I sure am glad you showed up. I really enjoyed our last adventure. Where are we going tonight?"

"Well," he said, "I just happened to notice that you were reading the story of Adam and Eve in your Bible before you went to sleep. How about we go see how they were created?"

"Sounds good to me," I replied.

As we glided into the Garden of Eden I noticed this garden looked nothing like my dad's garden.

The first thing I noticed was that there were no weeds anywhere.

"Hey Andy! How come I don't see any weeds?" I asked.

"Because they haven't been created yet."

"When were they created?"

"When God cursed the ground after Adam and Eve sinned."

"So that's where weeds and thorns come from?"

"Yep."

I had more questions about weeds, but I noticed something else that distracted me. "How come these mosquitoes aren't biting me?" I asked.

"Because at this point in creation, everything was perfect," he replied.

And he was right! I noticed that everything *was* perfect… and beautiful.

I didn't see any dead leaves or dead limbs on any of the trees. None of the apples in the nearby apple tree were rotten or had any worm holes in them.

I remembered once when dad took our family to the apple orchard to get some fresh apples. He let me pick one right off the tree to eat. And when I bit into it, I saw a little brown tunnel in the apple, where I had just taken a bite. I asked dad what it was, and he said it was a worm hole.

Then dad asked me, "What is worse than finding a worm in your apple?"

I didn't know the answer because I thought nothing could be worse than finding a worm in my apple.

Then he said, "Finding half a worm!"

Yuck! I knew what that meant. That meant the other half of the worm was in my belly!

"Shhhh," said Andy. "Look who is coming."

We hid behind a tree, and watched as God came walking through the garden. And guess what God was doing? He was talking to Himself.

Yep! Just like dad does when he thinks no one is around.

Andy and I leaned in closer so that we could hear what He was saying.

"Let's see, I have created day and night. I have separated the land and the water. I have made the grass and the trees. And I have created the stars and all the planets. I have created fish in the seas and birds to fly through the air. What else? Oh yes! I created all of the other creatures that will live on the earth and I have made it so that they will all have babies. What a great idea, that baby thing!"

And then God stopped. He looked all around. Then He bragged on Himself. "I did good," He said.

Then it was as if God was thinking of something else.

"But none of these creatures can talk," He continued. "I sure would like to have someone here on earth that I could talk to."

"I know! I'll make another creature, only this one will be different than all of the other creatures I have created. This creation will look like Me!"

And then Andy and I watched in amazement as God knelt down and began gathering dirt in a big pile in front of Him. I don't know how He did it, because I didn't see Him mix the dust with water, but somehow the dust began to stick together. It was the coolest thing ever!

All of a sudden Andy started to get up like he was going to walk over to God. I grabbed him by the shoulder and pulled him back down. "What are you doing?" I asked quietly.

"I've seen you do this with play dough," Andy said. "And it always looked fun. So I thought maybe God will let me play with Him," he whispered.

"What? *Play with God*? Are you CRAZY?"

"Sure. Why not?"

"Because, He's God!"

"I know Who He is. I've been in heaven with Him for a long time."

"Oh yeah, I forgot. But do you really think God has a sense of humor?"

"Well of course He does!"

"Why do you think that?"

"Have you seen some of the creatures He created?"

"Like what?"

"Look at that one over there. It's the ugliest four legged thing I have ever seen. And listen to it. It laughs!!!"

"Yeah, it's called a laughing hyena," I said.

"What about that really tall creature, with long skinny legs peeking over the top of that tree?"

"That's a giraffe," I said.

"What about that one with the big red behind?"

Laughing, I replied, "That is a baboon. You're right. God really does have a great sense of humor."

"But be quiet. I want to see what else God is doing," I said.

We watched intently. The dust and dirt in God's hands began to take on a magical form. In God's hands plain ole dust and dirt were being formed into something beautiful.

And then I saw something happening. The look on God's face began to change. As this creation was being formed in His hands, I saw on His face that same look that my mom gives to me when I give her a big hug.

It was love! Unconditional love! Love that goes beyond words!

Suddenly the song that we sing in Kid's Church made complete sense. *Jesus loves me this I know. For the Bible tells me so.*

As I watched the passion and intensity on God's face it made tears start to well up in my eyes. *Wow*, I thought, *this means that God really does love me.*

And I also realized something else. When God made all of the animals He *spoke* them into existence. But not man! With loving care and with His own hands He *formed* man. And just like my dad smiles real big when someone tells him I look like him... I saw that same smile coming over God's face as He put the finishing touches on this man He was forming from the dust.

And then God really surprised me. He leaned down over this man He had created, and blew into his nose!

I'm not kidding! God blew right into his nose!

All I could think of was... *I hope this guy doesn't sneeze right now!!!*

Andy leaned over and said with a snicker, "Hey! Look Matthew. God is blowing his nose"!

Have you ever been somewhere where you know you should be acting all serious? But for some reason you got the giggles? And the more you tried to stop laughing, the more you laughed?

We took turns shushing each other but just about the time I would get it under control Andy would give me that goofy look of his and off I would go again.

I thought for sure God was going to hear us and turn and scold us!

That reminded me of the time mom and dad made me go to a funeral with them. There was a lady and her son sitting in front of us. The kid looked about my age. I watched as the kid licked the palm of his hand. Then he rubbed it real hard until it was dry. Then he smelled it.

His mom noticed him smelling his hand and I'm not sure what he told her, but she held her own hand up to her nose and smelled her own hand.

And then, as quick as a rabbit, he whacked the bottom of her hand and she smacked herself right in the nose!

I knew I shouldn't be laughing at a funeral, and I knew I shouldn't be laughing at someone getting hit on the nose, but I couldn't help it! And it wasn't just one of those little snicker laughs. I laughed so hard I snorted! My mom elbowed me real hard in the ribs and told me to "Shut it!"

But I couldn't.

It ended up with me and the other kid both getting a few swats from both of our moms at the same time! Yep, I finally stopped laughing.

So there Andy and I were, in the Garden of Eden. And God is doing some pretty serious stuff, like breathing life into Adam. And we can't stop laughing.

But then I remembered our pastor preaching about how sometimes God has to discipline people. And the quick thought of God bending me of His knee and giving me a few swats sobered me right up!

Andy must have read my mind because he stopped laughing too.

As soon as God blew His breath into the nostrils of the man He had created, it was like that scene from the old black and white movie about Frankenstein.

Slowly the man began to breath. Then he opened his eyes. Then he began to wiggle his fingers. Then he moved his legs.

And then he leaped to his feet!

The coolest thing was, he knew how to walk and talk right away. He didn't have to *learn* anything!

At that moment Andy pulled on my shirt sleeve and said, "Hey Matthew, it's time to go."

As I climbed aboard Andy's back I heard God and Adam talking and laughing. It reminded me of how my dad likes to make me laugh.

The dream ended and I woke up in my bed. And again I lay there looking out my bedroom window.

The full moon was so bright it almost looked daylight outside. And there in the moonlight was the old oak tree in our back yard.

There was a gentle breeze that was moving the branches and the leaves back and forth. And in that moment I remembered a conversation that I heard my dad have with Grandpa.

My dad had asked Grandpa how was it that scientist could have found rocks and fossils in the earth that appeared to look millions of years old, when according to the Bible the earth is only about six thousand years old.

And Grandpa responded by asking my dad a question. He asked, "When God created everything on creation day, did He plant seeds and wait for trees to grow? Did He create the earth flat, and wait for nature, and the wind and water to create the mountains and valleys?"

"No," said Grandpa, answering his own question. "He created full grown trees. He spoke and mountains and valleys were formed. God created a mature creation!"

It clicked in my mind. I had just witnessed in my dream how that Adam, the man that God created in the Garden of Eden, was created as a full grown man. He wasn't born. He was created! He wasn't formed as a baby. He was formed as a mature man that already knew how to everything a mature man would do.

And the same thing happened with Eve. When God took the rib from Adam's side He created a full grown woman. He didn't create a baby girl and then wait for her to grow up!

The same was true with all of the animals. God didn't create eggs and then wait for them to hatch. Everything that was created had the *appearance* of being much older than it actually was.

And if all of the trees, mountains, animals, and even Adam and Eve were created to look much older than they actually were, wouldn't the same be true with the earth itself?

The rocks, along with their fossils, were created to look much older than they actually are.

So of course archeologists are going to think the earth is much older than it truly is. But that's because it was created to look and act that way!

★ ★ ★ ★

But laying there in my bed, after waking from my dream, I suddenly became a little sad for Adam and Eve. It dawned on me that they missed out on what it was like to be a little kid.

And what better place could a kid have grown up than the Garden of Eden? Here was a place that was full of animals! Dogs, cats, rabbits, and every other kind of animal imaginable. It would have been like living at the zoo. There had to have been so many things to do and see! It would have been like living in a fairy tale story.

Well… God did call it "paradise"!

As I continued laying there looking at the full moon shining on our old oak tree, I had one last thought before I drifted back off to sleep. My dad always grins when someone tells him that I look just like him.

So it is no wonder God loves us so much. We were created in His likeness. We were created in His image. Therefore God looks upon us with great love because He is our Heavenly Father and we are His children. And

I'm sure God smiles when one of the angels tells Him that one of His children looks just like Him!

Discuss the following questions with your parents or a friend:

- Why didn't Matthew and Andy get any mosquito bites?
- When did Andy want to play with God?
- What happened to cause Adam to take his first breath?
- How big were the first trees that God made?
- What word did Matthew's grandpa use to describe creation? (M _ _ _ _ _)

CHAPTER 3: HISS....

Now I knew what to expect in my dreams.

Andy came swooping down into my bedroom and this time I thought I'd try something different.

I waved my index finger in a circle in the air. Andy caught on immediately. Instead of landing he flew right on by and made a big swoop in the air. Then he circled back. He slowed down slightly... and I JUMPED! Yep! I was going to try to jump aboard as he flew by! I landed on his back but my momentum pushed me all the way around his back. Suddenly I found myself under Andy... face to face... and I was hanging on for dear life!

Did you know that angels are ticklish? Well, I'm not sure about all angels, but Andy sure is! And for me to hang on I had to grab ahold of him right under his wings which was his tickle spot!

Have you ever tried to run while you are laughing? Now imagine trying to *fly* while you are laughing! I thought for sure we were going to crash!

Andy finally reached down and grabbed both of my wrists with his hands and pulled me loose from hanging onto him. I felt like I was 3 years old again and my dad was holding my hands and swinging me around in circles!

We quickly made an emergency landing, and I climbed back onto his back.

Once I was securely on his back I asked, "What are we going to see this time?"

"Do you like snakes?"

"Only if they are at the zoo and behind the thick glass."

"Sorry, this one is not in a zoo. It's probably the meanest snake you will be meet!"

"Worse than a rattlesnake?"

"Much worse!"

"Worse than a cobra?"

"Much, much worse!"

Needless to say I was very apprehensive as we glided into the Garden of Eden.

I heard someone saying… "Elephants… monkeys… horses… cows…" and on and on he went.

It was Adam and he was naming all of the animals that God had created. He sure was intelligent! He was coming up with names I had never heard of.

I told Andy, "This scene sure does not match what is in my school textbook."

"What do you mean?" he asked.

"My science textbook has pictures of what they think the first man looked like. According to them, the first man looked a lot like an ape. And not only did he look like an ape, he was as dumb as an ape."

Andy responded, "Well, clearly Adam did not look like an ape. And instead of being simple minded like a monkey or an ape, he was highly intelligent!"

"Dogs… cats… seals…" Then Adam stopped naming names. "Oh, hi God!" he said.

"Hi Adam! How do you like the job I gave you of naming all the animals?"

"Okay I guess. But do you mind if I ask a question?"

"Sure, go right ahead," replied God.

"I noticed something today. You created some really goofy looking animals!"

God laughed. Yes. God actually laughed!

"You are right," God said. "But I find beauty in every animal I created regardless of their shape, or color! I also see worth in every creature whether they are as smart as a dolphin, or as dumb as a donkey!"

A song we sing in Kids Church came to my mind… *Red and yellow, black or white, They are precious in His sight, Jesus loves the little children of the world.*

Adam continued, "There is one other question I would like to ask."

"Ask away," said God.

"I noticed that for every animal I have named, each one has a mate. However, I do not have a mate."

"You are absolutely right," replied God, scratching His chin. "Let's do something about that."

Then God told Adam to lie down. God waved His hand over Adam, and immediately he fell into a deep sleep.

Wow! I thought, *maybe God will do that for me the next time I have to go to the dentist!*

Then God took a rib bone from Adam's side. And with that single bone in His hands God knelt in the dust and started to form Eve the same way He created Adam.

Grinning real big, Andy tapped me on the shoulder. "Do you think Adam checked the place on his driver's license to be a organ donor?"

Sometimes Andy just kills me with his off-the-wall sense of humor!

☆☆☆☆

Then something happened in my dream. We jumped forward in time.

A *Time Jump*.

We were still in the Garden of Eden, but I could tell that some time had passed.

"Here He comes," Adam was saying to Eve.

I could tell by the look on their faces, whoever was coming was someone they cared deeply for.

Then, there in the cool of the evening, God appeared in the garden.

"Well, how did it go today?" God asked.

"Great," said Adam, "We gave names to four or five hundred more animals today."

On and on they chatted. Sometimes their conversation was interrupted with laughter as they talked to God about what happened during the day.

And then God's voice took on a more serious tone.

"Listen closely to what I am getting ready to tell you. You may eat the fruit of every tree in the garden except the tree that is located in the middle of the garden. Do you know which tree I am talking about?" God asked.

"Yes sir!" said Adam and Eve in unison.

"I mean it! You are never to eat any of the fruit on that tree. You may eat of all of the other trees, but not that one. Are we clear?"

Again Adam and Eve said, "Yes sir!" in unison.

After saying, "good night," God left the garden.

Then I experienced another *Time Jump.*

Suddenly, again in my dream, it was some time later. And Andy and I were there in the garden.

However, I could sense immediately that something was wrong.

Once I walked into Grandma and Grandpa's house and I could tell that something was wrong. Grandpa was leaned back in his recliner and Grandma was rocking back and forth in her rocking chair. The TV was turned off and neither one of them was talking. And not only that, they wouldn't even look at each other.

And it was quiet!

I didn't like how it felt, so I went back home and told mom about it. She said not to worry. They were just having a disagreement about something but they would work it out. She said they always worked their problems out.

I now felt that same awkwardness in the Garden of Eden.

It just felt bad. I could tell something was not right.

I could feel the presence of something bad. Even though the sun was shining, there was an overwhelming feeling of darkness.

Eve was on her knees and gently singing as she admired the beauty of the thousands of flowers growing throughout the garden. Adam was lying on the ground with his back up against a tree, just relaxing.

Looking back now I don't know why they did not flee from that evil spirit as soon as it entered the garden.

But I have to admit to one thing. That evil being was beautiful to look at. He flew into the garden with an attitude of arrogance and pride, just like he owned the place.

Everything about him shouted defiance.

"Did I overhear God tell you that you could not eat of the tree that is in the middle of the garden?" Satan asked Eve.

"Yes," she replied. "In fact He told us that not only should we not eat of the tree, but we are not even allowed to touch it. He said that if we did, we would die."

"Die? What do you mean… die??? Have you ever seen anything die? Surely you will not die! Did He tell you why you were not allowed to eat of that tree?"

"No," replied Eve. "All I know is that He said we should not eat of any of the fruit that grows on it."

"Did you know that I used to live in heaven with God?"

"Really?" replied Adam.

"I sure did. But He kicked me out of heaven!"

"What did He do that for?" asked Adam.

"I think He was getting jealous of me, so He kicked me out of heaven. But never mind all of that. You do know the real reason God does not want you to eat of the tree don't you?"

"Why?" asked Eve.

"Because He knows that if you eat of the tree you shall become like Him, knowing the difference between good and evil."

I wanted to jump up and down and scream out at Eve. "*He* is the one that is evil! Don't listen to him!"

The devil continued in a tempting voice, "Come on, let's go look at the tree and see if it looks like it will hurt you."

Eve stood up and walked over to the tree.

"It doesn't look like it will hurt me" she said. "In fact the fruit looks absolutely delicious."

"Come on," said Satan, "Surely one little bite won't hurt anything!"

I recalled the words that I heard Miss Murphy, my Sunday school teacher say, "Flee from the very appearance of evil".

And again I wanted to scream out at Eve to run away from this evil being.

Slowly Eve reached out her hand… closer and closer… to the piece of fruit that was hanging there in the sunlight.

If only I were allowed to interfere with people in my dreams I would have shouted as loud as I could, "Stop it! Don't do it!"

Now her hand was on the piece of fruit. She tugged. The stem snapped as the piece of fruit broke loose from the limb.

Ever so slowly she raised the fruit to her lips.

As soon as she took the first bite she turned to Adam who was now there beside her.

"He's right. It tastes delicious. Here, you take a bite!"

And Adam also took a bite.

However, the look on their faces immediately began to change.

Gone was their innocence.

They had sinned! And suddenly, they realized that now there were going to be consequences to pay.

Adam looked at Eve and Eve looked at Adam. And they both realized they were not wearing clothes.

I could see it in their faces. They were thinking, "Oh no! What have we done?"

They ran over to a nearby fig tree and pulled leaves from the tree and sewed them together to make clothes for themselves.

Then they heard the footsteps of God as He came walking into the garden to spend time talking with them in the cool of the evening.

They quickly ran and hid behind some bushes.

"Where are you?" God cried out.

And Adam and Eve tried to hide even more.

"Adam and Eve… where are you?" called out God again.

Adam finally spoke up. "We heard You in the garden but we were afraid to talk to You."

"Why are you afraid?"

"Because we're naked."

"Who told you that you were naked? There is only one way you would know that you were naked. Did you eat of the tree that was forbidden?"

"Yes," replied Adam. "Eve ate from the tree and she gave it to me and I ate from it as well."

"What have you done?" cried out the Lord. "What have you done?"

"It's the evil serpent's fault" replied Eve. "He tricked me! He gave it to me and I ate it".

Again I wanted to shout out in my dream. I wanted to tell God that she was not telling the truth. The serpent didn't give it to her. She was the one that took the fruit from the tree.

The sinful nature of lying and deceit that was in Satan immediately became part of Eve's nature. The same way the serpent deceived her she now was trying to deceive God.

Again I remembered something I heard Pastor Mark say. *Sin will take you places you did not want to go, and keep you longer than you planned to stay!*

God turned to Adam and Eve and said, "Because you have done this you must leave the Garden of Eden. And now because of sin, I have to place several curses on My creation."

Then God cursed the form that Satan had taken. He told the serpent that he would be lower than all of the other creatures he had created. He said "You will crawl on your belly and eat dust all the days of your life."

He turned to Adam and Eve and told them there would now be problems between man and woman. And He said there will now be problems between parents and their children.

And then He spoke of things to come. He said that He would crush Satan's head and he would strike His heel.

Then God turned to Eve and told her that because of her sin she would have great pain when she gave birth to her children. And he said, "You now must submit to your husband, he will now rule over you."

Then God turned to Adam and said, "Because you took the fruit from Eve, and because you disobeyed Me, the ground is now cursed because of you and you will have to work hard to eat of the fruit of the ground all the days of your life."

"Not only that," said God, "but the ground will produce thorns and thistles, and the only way you will be able to eat is to weed out those things. You will have to work hard and it will cause you to sweat."

Then God told them that the final curse was that mankind would return to dust when he died.

I thought, "Wow, God sure is upset! I bet He just turns and walks away from Adam and Eve and never talks to them again."

But then God did something amazing. He gently took the life of one of the animals there in the garden. And He used the skin of the slain animal to make clothes for Adam and Eve.

With great love and great tenderness He placed the clothes He had made on Adam and Eve to cover their nakedness.

I jolted awake.

I lay there thinking about what I had just seen in my dream.

I became very much aware of how it hurt God when I sinned. Every time I sin, every time I tell a lie, and every time I try to deceive my mom and dad it reminds God of that day in the garden when Adam and Eve not only broke the law of God, but they also broke the heart of God.

And it also made me realize that that is why it is hard for me to pray when I know I have done something that is against the Word of God. Sin breaks that fellowship between me and God.

After I do something wrong, I am so ashamed that I don't want to talk to God, the same way Adam and Eve tried to hide from God after they sinned.

But something else also made sense to me now. The same way God offered up the life of that animal in the garden to cover Adam and Eve's nakedness and sin, God offered up the life of Jesus, His Son, to suffer and die to cover my sin.

"It's no wonder people are afraid of snakes," I thought. Now every time I see a snake it will remind me that Satan is a liar and a deceiver and I should never listen when he tries to talk to me.

I decided every time I hear the devil's voice I will just stick my fingers in my ears and respond with a "Hissss!"

Discuss the following questions with your parents or a friend:

- How smart was Adam?
- Who kicked Satan out of heaven, and why?
- Who ate of the tree in the middle of the garden first?
- How many curses can you remember that were a result of Adam and Eve's sin?

CHAPTER 4: A BUNCH OF OLD DUDES

"**A** re you ready for another trip?" asked Andy.

"*Another dream and another adventure?*"

"Yes!" I shouted.

I couldn't wait to see what Andy had in mind tonight.

"How old are your great grandparents?"

"I think they are in their eighties," I replied. "All I know is that they are really old!"

"So you think someone in their eighties is really old, huh?"

"Yes. Grandpa has to use a cane to get around. And Grandpa and Grandma's skin is all wrinkly and saggy. All that loose skin looks funny. And sometimes I like flipping the loose skin that hangs down under grandpa's arms. It's almost like he has wings!"

"How would you like to meet someone that is ten times older than your grandparents?" asked Andy.

"Yeah right! What is it an Egyptian mummy?"

"No, just some really old people."

"Okay," I said. "I guess I'm game."

"Then all aboard for a trip to see some old dudes."

And off we flew.

"We are going to see some of the ancestors of Adam and Eve today."

"Okay," I responded.

"See that old dude over there?"

"Yep."

"Guess how old he is?"

"From the looks of him, he looks even older that my grandpa."

"He is! He is one hundred and thirty years old!"

"Wow! That is old!"

"Just wait. You haven't seen anything yet. See that old guy over there? Do you know who that old dude is?"

"No," I replied.

"That is Adam."

"The same Adam that we visited in the Garden of Eden?"

"Yep! But listen to this. Even though he and Eve are one hundred and thirty years old they are just now getting ready to start having a family."

At that time I knew that babies came from the mommy's belly but I wasn't quite sure how they got there. One of my friends at school said babies come from the mommy's belly button.

Thinking of Grandma I did the math in my head real quick.

"So Eve didn't start having babies until she was fifty years older than my grandma is right now?"

"Yep!" replied Andy.

"I guess that would work out okay. If Grandma's skin on her belly is as stretchy as her arms I guess the skin on Eve's belly would stretch out real nice when her belly started growing!"

I could tell by the strange look on Andy's face he couldn't believe I was talking about the skin on my grandma's belly.

Then we did the *time jump* thing again. We left that time period and jumped to another place in time.

★ ★ ★ ★

"Guess who this really old dude is?" asked Andy.

"He looks familiar but I have never seen anyone that looks *that* old."

"That is Adam. It's now been eight hundred years since the last time we saw him when he was one hundred and thirty years old."

"No way!"

"Yes. Today Adam is celebrating his nine hundred and thirtieth birthday!"

"Wow! What gift do you get for someone that is nine hundred and thirty years old?"

Andy grinned, "I don't know! But stand back when they get ready to light the nine hundred and thirty candles on his birthday cake!"

"Yeah! Should we go ahead and call the fire department now?" I laughed.

"See that other old dude?" Andy asked.

"Yes."

"That is Adam and Eve's first son. His name is Seth. And he is going to live to be nine hundred and twelve years old!"

"Wow! Let me ask this, who is the oldest dude ever to live?"

"That would be a guy name Methuselah. He lived to be nine hundred and sixty nine years old."

"When did people stop living so long?" I asked.

"Around the time Noah built the ark. God decided to shorten the years that man would live because they had become so evil."

"Are you ready to head back home?" Andy asked.

"I guess so," I said.

✦ ✦ ✦ ✦

The next day I went to visit my Grandma and Grandpa. I must have had a weird look on my face, because Grandma asked if there was something wrong.

I told her, "Nope. Everything is great. But you and Grandpa sure do look much younger today!"

After seeing those old dudes that were over nine hundred years old, Grandma and Grandpa looked pretty young!

Grandma grabbed me and gave me the biggest hug she has ever given to me. She squeezed me so tight I could hardly breathe.

When I left an hour later she was still grinning from ear to ear!

Discuss the following questions with your parents or a friend:

- How old were Adam and Eve when they had their first baby?
- Who was the oldest man in the Bible?
- How come people don't live as long as they did in the beginning of time?

CHAPTER 5: THE BIG BOAT

What's the biggest boat you have ever been on?" asked Andy as we took off for another adventure.

"My uncle Charles has a pontoon boat," I said. "And it's pretty big."

"If you were to walk from the front of your uncle's boat to the back, how many steps would you take?" asked Andy.

I thought about it a few seconds. "Probably about ten steps," I replied.

"So his boat is probably around twenty feet long. Would you like to see a boat that is four hundred and fifty feet long, seventy feet wide, and forty five feet tall?"

"You betcha!" I exclaimed.

"Then… all aboard!" Andy yelled out.

I jumped onto his back and off we went for our fifth adventure.

When we arrived we didn't land right away. Instead Andy flew several big circles around the boat so I could get a real good look at it.

It was the biggest boat I had ever seen. It was bigger than the football field where the high school kids play football!

"What a cool boat," I said.

"It's called an ark," said Andy.

I had heard our kids ministry leader, Miss Murphy, tell the story of Noah and the Ark but I did not realize the ark was this big!

"This is even bigger than the big church downtown!" I exclaimed.

"I know about this story," I said to Andy. "God sent the flood because the people stopped praying before they ate their meals, praying before they went to sleep at night, and they stopped going to church."

"Well, that's kind of what happened," replied Andy. "Have you ever heard of the word evil?"

"Yes, but I'm not sure I fully understand exactly what it means."

"Who is the meanest person you know?" asked Andy.

"Oh, that would be Carl! He will wait until the teacher isn't looking and then he will do something mean to whoever is around him. Last week he shot a spit wad right into Emily's mouth!"

"Eww," said Andy. "That is pretty mean… and gross! But I want you look at the men over there." Andy pointed to a bunch of men that were standing near the ark.

As soon as I looked at them I quickly looked for a place to hide.

They were the ugliest and meanest looking men I had ever seen! There was something about the way they talked and acted that made goose bumps jump up on my arms and made the little hairs on the back of my neck felt like they were standing up straight!

"Those men are evil," Andy stated.

"Yep, they sure are the meanest looking men I have ever seen." I replied.

Andy spoke up. "The Bible says these men were so wicked and mean that they had evil thoughts all the time. They never ever had good thoughts… ever."

He continued. "They were so evil that it made God's heart sad. In fact, God grew so sad that He finally decided to send a great flood and get rid of all the bad people on the earth."

"All except for Noah and his family, right?" I asked.

"Yes. God looked at all of the people that were on the earth, and the only good people left were Noah and his family."

"And God told Noah that He was going to send a great flood on the earth, but He told Noah how to build this big boat to save Noah's family and some of the animals that God had created," I said.

"Yes," Andy said, "And today is the day when all the animals are going to go into the ark."

And sure enough, just like Andy said, all kinds of animals starting walking toward the ark.

For some of the animals there were only two of each kind. Andy said that these were animals that were considered un-clean; therefore they were not to be used for food. But, Andy continued, there were seven of each kind of clean animals. He said the clean animals could be used for food.

We stood what seemed like for hours as we watched animals of all shapes and sizes enter the ark. There were pretty ones… ugly ones… fat ones… skinny ones… tall ones and short ones.

"How do they know to enter the ark?" I asked.

"Have you ever seen geese flying south when the weather turns cold?" asked Andy.

"Yes."

"How do they know which direction to fly?"

"I don't know. I guess they have a built in compass?"

"Actually they do have a built in compass. God also gave them a built in weather detector that tells them winter is coming and lets them know to fly south to escape the cold winter weather," said Andy. "And God gave that same instinct to all of these animals that are entering the ark."

"So they have their own GPS?"

"Yep. Only instead of GPS standing for *Global Positioning System*, it stands for *God Positioning System*," Andy said with a big grin.

"So God did the same thing with all these animals? He let them know they needed to enter the ark to be saved."

"He sure did."

"I once heard Pastor Mark say God has put something inside of every boy and girl that tells them that they need to be saved."

"That is right," said Andy. "You might call it a moral compass. Mankind was born with the desire to want to know God."

Andy and I watched as all of the animals marched onto the ark.

"Hey Andy, how come the dogs are not chasing the cats? And how come the lions are not chasing the deer? None of these animals are attacking each other like they do on the safari TV show?"

Andy smiled and patted me on the head, "It looks like God can turn your enemy into a friend, doesn't it?"

Immediately I thought of Carl, the mean kid in my class.

Andy must have known what I was thinking. "Just wait a few years. Don't be surprised if Carl doesn't end up being one of your best friends!" he said.

"Ha!" I replied. "Fat chance of that!"

Little did I know that Andy was (or would be) 100% right in the future.

Andy picked up a wooden hammer and a long spike that Noah used for nails.

"I have always thought I would make a good carpenter," he said, looking at me as he starting nailing it into a board.

"You had better pay attention to what you're doing," I told him.

No sooner had I got those words out of my mouth and *pow*! Andy hit his thumb with the hammer. Immediately his thumb swelled up twice its normal size and turned bright red! I know I shouldn't have laughed at him, but it was funny!!!

"Look Andy! Now your thumb matches your hair!"

★ ★ ★ ★

There is a man that goes to our church that raises cows. One Saturday morning dad took me to his farm. We got there just in time to see him feeding the cows. I could hardly believe how much they could eat.

And now as I watched all of those large animals entering the ark I couldn't help but wonder how Noah was going to feed them?

"How long will everyone have to stay aboard the ark?" I asked Andy.

"For almost a year." Andy replied.

"A year?"

"Yes. Almost a full year."

"Then a big part of the ark must be like a barn... all full of hay and food for the animals?"

"Yes. Noah really had to think about what it was going to take, to take care of all of those animals".

"That sounds like fun!" I said.

"Well... let's stop and think about that," Andy replied.

"Who is going to have to feed all of those animals?"

"My guess is Adam is going to give that job to his sons."

"That sure sounds like a lot of work."

"Do you remember the hamster you received for your birthday?" Andy asked.

"Yes."

"And do you remember how your dad told you that if you got a hamster you had to take care of it?"

"Yes."

"Do you remember cleaning its cage every day?"

"Yes! I didn't know a hamster that little could poop so much!"

Andy just remained silent.

He looked at me. I looked at him.

"What?" I asked.

"You only had one little hamster cage to clean. Think about it!"

Then I got it!

"Oh my goodness!" I exclaimed. "Who do you think had to clean up after the elephants!?!" I shouted!

"My guess is that Noah also gave that stinky job to his sons!"

"Yep! That is exactly what my dad would have done!!!"

Andy looked at me. And I looked at Andy. We were both thinking the same thing. That ark must have had a really bad odor.

I grabbed my nose. Andy grabbed his nose. Then both of us doubled over with laughter at the thought of that much poop!

✳ ✳ ✳ ✳

"Do you remember how Noah knew it was safe for everyone to leave the ark?" asked Andy.

"Yes."

Then I told Andy how Noah had released a dove to see if the water had gone down enough for the dove to find a place to land. But the dove returned to the ark. And Noah did this day after day until the dove returned with an olive leaf in its beak. And then, after waiting seven more days, Noah opened the door and let everyone out.

"I bet everyone sure was glad to breathe some fresh air, don't you?" I asked Andy.

"I bet so too!"

"Can you imagine how bad that ark must have smelled after almost a year with only one door and one window?" I asked Andy.

I remembered being in the truck with Grandpa one time, and even though I didn't hear anything, it suddenly started to smell bad. And then Grandpa started laughing!

"Real funny, Grandpa!" I hollered.

I held my nose until I could roll down the window and let in some fresh air!

If they had them… I bet Noah and his family wore nose plugs most of the time.

"Do you remember the promise that God made to Noah after the flood?" asked Andy.

"I sure do. God sent a rainbow as a promise that He would never again send this kind of destruction against the earth."

"Correct," replied Andy.

Once again I found myself back home all safe and sound in my bed. I lay there thinking about what it must have been like for Noah and his family to be cooped up inside the ark for almost a year.

I rolled out of bed and opened my bedroom window. In came a gentle fresh breeze blowing the curtains from side to side.

I breathed deeply and thought about just how challenging it must have been for Noah and his family on the ark. Andy and I may have laughed about it for a few minutes but I realized it was not funny at all to Noah and his family.

And then a verse from the Bible came to my mind… *Let everything that has breath praise the Lord!*

Once more I breathed deeply as the fresh air came flowing in through the window. Then I did just what that scripture said… I lifted both of my hands and gave praise and thanks to the Lord for all of the wonderful things He had given to me.

I thanked Him for my Mom and Dad, my pastor, my church, and my friends. I thanked Him for providing me with food, clothes, and a safe place to live. Then I thanked Him for sending His Son, Jesus, to take away my sins and for the promise of eternal life with Him.

Then I drifted off to sleep. It seems like it is easier to go to sleep after I have said my bedtime prayers.

Discuss the following questions with your parents or a friend:

- How big was the ark?
- How many of each clean animal were allowed on the ark?
- How long did Noah and his family stay on the ark?
- What type of bird came back with an olive leaf in its beak?

CHAPTER 6: FATHER ABRAHAM

Do you want to go see Abraham?" asked Andy.

"Abraham Lincoln?" I asked.

"No. The Abraham in the Bible that is also known as 'Father Abraham'"

"Sure. We sing about him in Kids Church. He is the one that had many sons, right?"

"Well, he ended up with a lot of sons, but that is not how it started. We need to go back to the beginning where God gave Abraham a promise."

"Yes" I said, "I've heard about the promise that God gave to him. He was told by God to leave where he lived and go on a trip, and that God would bless him and make him the father of many nations. But, I've got a question for you."

"Ask away."

"So God told Abraham to pack up and move but He didn't tell him where he was moving to, right?"

"Correct."

"Can you imagine what Sarah must have said when Abraham told her that they were moving, but he didn't know where?"

Then Andy started imitating Abraham and said in his deepest voice. "Uhhh. Hey Sarah! Pack up everything we own, we are getting ready to move."

Then Andy switched to a fake high woman's voice, "Why are we moving and where are we moving to?"

"God told me to move but He didn't tell me where."

"Are you kidding me? Why would God do that? That makes absolutely no sense! Are you sure it was God? You know how silly your dreams get after you eat spicy food!"

I started laughing because it made me remember the last time dad took us to a new restaurant. Dad had the address, and even though we had never been there before dad thought he could figure out how to get there.

Immediately we got lost. And we kept driving in circles. And even though we were lost, Dad refused to use our GPS or look at a map. We drove around in circles for what seemed like an hour.

And the whole time mom kept saying, "If you are not going to let me hook up the GPS at least pull over and ask for directions!"

And dad kept mumbling how he had a *God given sense of direction in his head.*

And mom kept mumbling something about dad being *as lost as a goose in a snow storm!*

Mom's face kept getting redder and redder and Dad started sweating a lot.

Dad finally gave in and told Mom to hook up the GPS. As it turned out we had been driving in circles around the restaurant the whole time!

✯ ✯ ✯

"Hey Andy, do you know what a GPS is?" I asked.

"I think so. Isn't it a gadget that tells you how to get somewhere?"

"Yep, it sure is. I think God gave one of them Abraham and his ancestors so they would be able to find the land that God promised to Abraham."

"Yeah, that makes sense to me," said Andy.

"Speaking of Abraham's children, do you know how old Abraham and Sarah, his wife, were when Sarah gave birth to their first child?" asked Andy.

"All I know is Miss Murphy said that they were really old," I answered.

"Well, they were older than your great grandma and great grandpa!" said Andy.

I couldn't help but think about what it was like when my great grandma and great grandpa used to baby sit me and my younger sister. Both of them were completely worn out after just a couple of hours!

I was having a hard times imagining what it would be like for someone as old as my great grandma and great grandpa to have a little baby to take care of all the time.

My great grandpa takes naps *all the time*! So if my grandma had a little baby to take care of, I guess she could put the baby and my grandpa down for their naps at the same time.

The only problem would be that Great Grandpa snores so loud I am sure it would wake the baby. Sometimes his snoring sounds like a train is coming through the house!

★ ★ ★ ★

"If you're ready, let's go see Abraham," said Andy.

"I'm ready!"

And off we went.

"Look out!" I shouted.

In mid-flight, Andy tipped over sideways as we flew around the cliffs of a mountain. I thought for sure we were going to crash into the mountain head on!

Last year on the fourth of July we went to see an air show where the Blue Angels were flying jets in formation. I loved watching as the jets turned sideways when the pilot made a quick turn.

I think Andy must have been to one of those air shows recently because that was exactly how he was flying.

Zoom! We went one direction!

And then… zoom… off we went in another direction!

My head was flopping all over the place!

When we finally landed and I hopped off of Andy's back I was completely dizzy. And there in both of my hands were two handfuls of feathers! Yep, I had plucked feathers right off of Andy's wings!

"Oh no!" I shouted. "Can you still fly without some of your feathers?"

"Sure," replied Andy. "Actually I don't need wings to fly."

"Really? I thought your wings were like bird's wings. And I know that birds can't fly without their wings."

"Well," said Andy, "I think God just gave angels wings because He likes the way they look. We are spiritual creatures, so we are not bound by gravity the same way you are. Therefore we don't really need our wings to fly."

"So you are kind of like Superman?" I asked.

"Well… yes… kind of," said Andy.

Then Andy tried to puff up his chest muscles to look like Superman. But all it did was make his belly stick out!

"Super Belly!" I shouted out.

"I'll show you super belly!" Then Andy belly bumped me so hard I landed on the seat of my pants.

Laughing and scrambling back to my feet I asked, "Where are we now?"

"We are on a mountain where we are getting ready to meet Abraham and Isaac, his son" said Andy.

"Are they going on a father-son camping trip?"

"They are going on trip but I don't think you would call it a camping trip?" replied Andy.

"Shhhh…" said Andy. "Let's just watch and see what happens."

The first person I saw was Isaac. On his back he was carrying a large stack of wood. Behind him was Abraham. In one hand he was carrying a container that had smoke coming out of the top. And in his other hand he held a long, sharp knife.

"Hey dad!" asked Isaac, "I know we are coming here to offer up a sacrifice to Jehovah God, but in the past we have always brought an animal with us to use for the sacrifice. How come we didn't bring an animal with us this time?"

Then with a silly smile Isaac asked, "Is your old age starting to get to you? Did you forget to bring a sacrifice? Mom says you would forget your head if it wasn't attached to your body."

Abraham's response was an abrupt "No!"

"Aw, come on old man," Isaac said again with a playful tone in his voice, "Just admit it. You forgot."

Again Abraham's voice was short and to the point. "No, I did not forget. God will provide a sacrifice."

Then Isaac stopped and looked closely at his father. He had seen his father before when he was serious. But this was a look he had not seen before.

"Are you okay, dad?"

"Yes! I'm okay! But can we just stop talking about it?"

"Sure thing," Isaac quietly replied.

Then Abraham and Isaac started gathering large stones and stacking them until that had built a stone altar. I could tell they had done this before.

Then they stacked the wood on top of the altar.

"Son, do you trust me?" Abraham asked.

"Of course I do, dad," Isaac replied.

"Hold out your hands."

Then Abraham took a piece of rope and tied Isaac hands together. Then he knelt down and tied his feet together.

"What are you doing?" Isaac said.

I could see fear starting to cross Isaac's face.

"Just trust me son, as I put my trust in God."

Too afraid to speak, now all Isaac could do was nod his head.

With tears streaming down his face Abraham picked his son up, and placed him on the stack of wood!

"What is he doing?" I whispered to Andy loudly. "Surely he's not going to set him on fire is he?"

Then Abraham did something that nearly blew my mind! He placed one hand on Isaac's forehead to hold his head down, and with the other hand he placed the blade of the long sharp knife across Isaac's throat!

Any time I am watching a movie with mom and dad and it starts getting scary or intense, my mom has to stand up. She gets so edgy she can't stay seated. Sometimes she will even go stand in the dining room and peek around the corner until the scene is over!

I felt that same way as Abraham lowered the knife to Isaac's throat. I couldn't bare to watch. I covered my eyes with both hands, peeking around my fingers. Surely he wasn't going to cut the throat of his only son!

Again I found myself wanting to interfere with the adventure that was unfolding before my very own eyes. It was all I could do to keep myself from jumping up and shouting out for Abraham to stop what he was doing!

And just as the blade of the knife touched the throat of Isaac, an angel spoke out with a loud voice from heaven and said, "Abraham, Abraham!"

And Abraham quickly lifted the blade from Isaac's throat, and replied, "Here I am!"

Then the angel said, "Do not lay your hand on the lad, or do anything to him, for now I know that you fear God, since you have not withheld your son, your only son, from Me."

Then there was a noise behind Abraham. He turned around, and there behind him was a ram caught in some bushes. Abraham took the knife that just seconds before was about to cut the throat of Isaac, and cut the ropes that bound Isaac's hands and feet, setting him free!

Both of them ran over to where the ram was caught in the bushes. They pulled it loose and carried it to the altar, where they sacrificed it to the Lord.

✯ ✯ ✯ ✯

"Are you ready to get out of here?" asked Andy.

"Am I ever?" I quickly replied.

The flight back was much slower and smoother. I could tell that Andy knew what I had just seen had shaken me up a bit.

"What are you thinking?" asked Andy.

"That was intense! Do you think Abraham would have really gone through with killing his only son?"

"Well, the Apostle Paul wrote about the great faith of Abraham in the book of Hebrews. And Paul said that Abraham's faith was so strong that he believed that if he did have to kill his son, God would raise him from the dead!"

I had to think about that as we glided along.

Then the term I had heard several people use when talking about Abraham made complete sense. Over and over I had heard him called "The Father of the faithful."

"Wow! That really took a lot of faith, didn't it?" I asked.

"Yep! It sure did."

✯ ✯ ✯ ✯

Andy dropped me off in my bedroom. And just as he was about to fly away I stopped him.

"Hey Andy! I have a question for you."

"Ask away," he said.

"That angel that spoke out Abraham's name and caused him to stop from cutting Isaac's throat… do you know him?"

"I sure do. All of us angels know each other."

"Well, do me a favor the next time you see him?"

"Sure!"

"Will you give him a high five for me the next time you see him!"

"Hey, I'll even do better than that. I'll give him a high five with my wings," Andy said with a big grin!

I lay there in my bed after awaking from my dream. For a long time I pondered the scene I had just witnessed.

I turned on my bed side light, and picked up my Bible. Then I looked up the word "faith" in the back of my Bible where it gives meanings to words. And there in Romans I found what I was looking for. In chapter four, verse eleven, I found the verse that said Abraham was the *father of those who believe.*

"Father Abraham... Father Abraham… Father Abraham…" I thought.

Yes! Now the *Father Abraham* song made perfect sense to me!

Since I am a believer that means Abraham is *my* father too!

I sat up in bed and began to sing…

Father Abraham had many sons… Had many sons… had Father Abraham… I am one of them… and so are you… So let's just praise the Lord…

After I finished singing I lay back down in my bed and snuggled up with my arms wrapped tightly around my pillow.

If I am a child of Father Abraham, that means God will provide for me the same way He provided for Abraham!

Now I know why mom and dad didn't let me watch scary movies. With the thoughts of a long sharp knife dancing in my head it was close to daybreak before I finally was able to go back to sleep.

Discuss the following questions with your parents or a friend:

- Who called out to Abraham and stopped him from sacrificing Isaac on the altar?
- What kind of animal was caught in the bushes?
- Fill in the blank. Abraham was called "The Father of the _____".

CHAPTER 7: TRICKING DAD

I'll let you pick out the candles for your dad's birthday cake," Mom said to me.

"Okay."

It was my dad's 40th birthday, and Mom was planning a surprise birthday party for him.

There were so many candles to pick from. At first I thought about getting the big "4", and big "0" candles. Then I saw the candles that were red, white and blue.

But then I saw the perfect candles… the trick candles. No matter how hard you blow, you can't blow them out!

The party was a big success. Dad didn't have a clue and was very surprised and very happy to have so many friends over to celebrate his birthday.

And the trick candles were a great success. I thought dad was going to hyperventilate from trying to blow the candles out. We laughed and laughed at him as his face turned red from blowing the candles so hard!

I love playing tricks on my dad. Sometimes I will go into his bathroom and move his razor to a different drawer. Or hide his shoes in Mom's closet.

One day Dad showed me the quarter trick. Secretly he had taken a quarter and rubbed the edge of the quarter with a lead pencil, so that the edge was all black.

Then he told me that he bet I could not roll the quarter from the top of my forehead, down my nose, and across my lips and down to my chin, without letting the quarter lose contact with my face.

After he tricked me into trying it he told me to go look at myself in the mirror. And there from the top of my forehead all the way down to my chin was a long black streak of pencil lead!

✫ ✫ ✫ ✫

"Hey Andy! Do you have a pencil on ya?" I asked in my next dream.
"No. Why do you need a pencil?"
"I was just going to show you a trick my dad showed me".
"Oh! So you like playing tricks on people, huh?"
"Yes, I sure do!"
I could see that Andy was thinking.
"Then let's go on another adventure," Andy said.
"Okay. Where are we going this time?"

"Well, since you like tricking people, I'll show you how Isaac played a trick on Abraham, his dad."

"Is it a real funny trick?" I asked.

"No. Actually it ended up being a really mean trick."

"Have you ever seen any of the old time cowboy movies?" asked Andy.

I hesitated, because I wasn't sure where Andy was going with this question.

"Sure. My great grandpa loves to watch old movies, and I like watching them with him," I replied.

"Have you ever seen the cowboy run and leap onto his horse?"

"Yes. That always looked like fun," I said.

"Pretend I am the horse and run and jump onto my back," challenged Andy.

"Okay!" I shouted.

I backed up and took a big run…

and just when I left my feet and was in midair… Andy ducked!

Over his back I went… head over heels!

Andy doubled over in laughter and fell to the ground. His freckled chubby cheeks were jiggling as his red curly hair bounced up and down!

I didn't even let him get up. I jumped right onto his back as he lay there on the ground laughing.

Without any hesitation he stood right up and away we flew on another adventure.

✫ ✫ ✫ ✫

"So this young man is the grandson of Abraham, and the son of Isaac?" I asked.

"Yes he sure is," replied Andy. "His name is Jacob."

"What is going on?" I asked.

Andy proceeded to tell me how Isaac and his wife, Rebekah, had twin sons named Jacob and Esau. There was competition between the two sons from the time they were born.

Esau was the older of the two. So according to tradition he was supposed to inherit the most when their father died.

Esau was Isaac's favorite son, while Jacob was Rebekah's favorite son.

"Have you heard the story of how Esau sold his birthright and inheritance for a bowl of soup?" asked Andy.

"Yes. Miss Murphy told us that story in Kids Church."

Then I proceeded to tell Andy the story.

"Esau came home from hunting and was very, very hungry. Jacob had made some soup and Esau wanted to eat some of the soup. Jacob told him he could have a bowl of the soup if he would give up his birthright and his inheritance. Esau agreed."

"You are correct," Andy spoke up, "And now Isaac, the father, is an old man, getting ready to die. Rebekah realizes that he is getting ready to give the blessing to Esau, but since Jacob is her favorite son she wants Jacob to receive the blessing. And that is where we come in today. Jacob and his mom are going to try to trick Isaac into giving the blessing to Jacob. Shhh…. here comes Rebekah and Jacob."

★ ★ ★ ★

"Here is the plan," Rebekah was saying to Jacob. "Your dad just told Esau to go hunting and bring home something to cook for him. When Jacob brings him the food, Isaac is going to give Esau the blessing. So if you are going to receive the blessing that Esau sold to you, we need to move quickly."

"But how are we going to trick him into giving me the blessing, when Esau and I are so different?" said Jacob. "We look different, we talk different, and we smell different."

"I know," said his mom, "but Isaac is almost blind, so all we have to do is make you smell and feel like Esau."

"I have an idea," Rebekah continued. "You go kill two goats and cook them the same way Esau does. Then when you take the food to him he will think you are Esau, and will give you the blessing."

"Surely Dad will be able to tell that it's me and not Esau. What if he reaches out and touches me? Esau is all hairy and my skin is smooth. If he catches me trying to trick him, I just know that he will bring a curse upon me instead of the blessing!"

"You take care of cooking the meal and leave the rest up to me," Rebekah responded.

Andy and I watched as Jacob quickly prepared the meal.

And all the while, Rebekah had gone into Esau's bedroom and gathered some of his clothes. Then she went outside and came back in with the skins of the two goats that Jacob had killed for the meal.

"Here. Wrap this goat skin around your neck. Now wrap some around your arms. Not only will you smell like Esau, but if Isaac touches you, your arms and neck will feel rough and hairy like Esau."

Jacob did like his mother said, and then took the meal to his father.

"Hey Dad, I have prepared the meal like you asked me to," Jacob lied, trying to disguise his voice to sound like Esau.

"That sure was quick. How did you go hunting, kill the prey, and fix a meal so quickly?" Isaac responded.

"The Lord gave me favor," replied Jacob, lying a second time.

Then Isaac said to Jacob, "Come on over here by my bed so I can touch you. I need to know that you truly are Esau."

Isaac reached out and touched the arms of Jacob that were covered with the goat skins. "You feel like Esau. But your voice sounds like the voice of Jacob," he said.

"Are you really Esau?" he questioned.

"Yes, I am," said Jacob, lying again.

"Then bring me the meal you have prepared, so I can bless you."

As Jacob set the meal in front of Isaac, Isaac said, "Come close my son, and give me a kiss."

As Jacob leaned down and kissed Isaac, Isaac smelled him.

"Yes, you smell like Esau."

I have often heard the phrase *dysfunctional family*. And that sure is what this appeared to be.

Here we had two brothers that were at odds with each other. We had a mother that favored one son, and the father that favored the other son. And now all of this dysfunction had led to this moment of trickery and deceit.

I felt so sorry for Isaac. Two of the people he loved the most were taking advantage of him.

"Shouldn't we try to do something about this?" I whispered to Andy.

"No. Do you remember Esau selling his birthright to Jacob for a bowl of soup?"

"Yes."

"Who do you think truly deserves the blessing and inheritance? Should it be someone that really appreciates it, or someone that was willing to give it all up for a trivial bowl of soup?"

"You make a good point," I replied. "But still yet, they are taking advantage of an old blind man."

I watched as Isaac pronounced the blessing over Jacob. In the blessing Isaac declared that the riches of heaven and earth would be Jacobs. He declared that nations would bow before Jacob and serve him. And that he would be the lord over all of his brothers and his mother. And then he finished the blessing by saying that those that bless him would be blessed, and those that curse him would be cursed.

As soon as the blessing was pronounced, Jacob quickly left the room because he knew that Esau would be showing up at any moment.

And sure enough, as soon as Jacob left, Esau showed up with his meal, only to find out that his father had already given the blessing to Jacob.

"Now what?" I asked Andy.

"Well, Jacob now has to leave the land because he is afraid his brother will kill him. But after several years he will return home, and everything will be okay."

"Is this where the saying *blood is thicker than water* came from?" I asked.

"I'm not sure. But it sure would apply in this situation, wouldn't it?"

"It sure would! I'm not sure I would be able to forgive someone if they did that to me."

"Well, as you continue to read through the book of Genesis, you will see that God used this situation, and it all turned out just fine," replied Andy.

After Andy dropped me back off in my bedroom, the first thing I did after waking up… was go back to dad's bathroom and put his razor back where it belonged. Somehow playing a trick on my dad didn't seem the right thing to do tonight!

Discuss the following questions with your parents or a friend:

- What did Esau sell his blessing for?
- How did Jacob trick his father?
- Who helped Jacob play the trick on his father?

CHAPTER 8: THE WRESTLING MATCH

One of me and my dad's favorite things to do is watch wrestling on TV.

It looks real to me, but dad laughs at me sometimes when I start taking it too seriously. He said that when the matches are over, all of the wrestlers are best friends.

In a way I kind of like that idea. All I can say is they sure make it look real!

Sometimes while we are watching wrestling on TV, with a mischievous grin on his face, dad will push me. And I will push him back.

The next thing you know we are down in the floor wrestling.

He calls me *Macho Matthew*. And I call him *Dangerous Daddio*!

It's a lot of fun. And I guess you would call mom the referee, because she always says the same thing. "You two had better stop it before somebody gets hurt."

And I always know who that "somebody" is. It's usually me!

Although one time we were wrestling around in the front room and I climbed up on the couch. Pretending I was standing on the top rope I dove off, landing on top of dad, hitting him right in his lower stomach! His face turned real red! His eyes scrunched all up! And he wiggled around on the floor like a fishing worm on our driveway when the concrete is very hot!

He was laughing, but I think he was laughing to cover up the pain.

Another time when we were wrestling, we accidentally knocked a vase off the shelf in the family room. It shattered into a million pieces. I thought for sure we were going to get in trouble!

Instead, mom started laughing… and laughing… and laughing.

I thought she was so mad she had lost her mind! But dad pulled me aside and said that it was a vase from Aunt Freda, and that mom had always hated the vase but she felt obligated to set it out for Aunt Freda to see when she popped in.

After mom cleaned up the mess she grabbed me and gave me the biggest hug ever! She must have really hated that vase!

Last night dad and I spent the evening watching wrestling.

And it must have still been on mind when I went to bed, because I started dreaming about being a professional wrestler.

I had flames painted on my face, and a long cape that had flames on it. There were flames on my tights, and flames on my shoes. And across the front of my shirt were two initials… *MM* … that stood for *Macho Matthew*!

I was announced as the *Champion Of The World*!

And I loved how the words echoed in my dreams.

Macho… acho… acho… Matthew… atthew… atthew…

Lights were flashing all over the stadium, and loud music was just a thumping. Thousands of people were on their feet chanting my name.

As I entered the ring I could not believe who was in the ring ready to fight me.

It was Andy!

"What in the world are you doing in my wrestling dream?" I shouted across the ring at him.

"I am here to take the championship belt from you!" he shouted back.

Thinking I would get the jump on him I charged across the ring at him.

But quick as a snap he flapped his little wings and up he went… quickly out of my reach.

He buzzed around the stadium and then came flying back into the ring headed straight at me! Suddenly the crowd stopped shouting out my name and started screaming out his name.

Awesome Andy! Awesome Andy!

Awesome… some… some… Andy… ndy… ndy!

And sure enough... there across the front of his shirt were the initials... *AA*!

However, instead of wrestling with me, he swooped down and picked me up and we flew right out the stadium double doors!

"What are you doing?" I shouted out as we flew out the doors and into the night.

"What do you think I'm doing? What do we do every time I show up in your dreams?" he said.

"All right! Another adventure!"

"Where are we going this time?" I asked.

"I thought since you were already dreaming about wrestling we would go see a wrestling match."

"Let me guess. Are we going to see *Goliath the Giant*?"

"Nope."

"How about *Samson the Slayer*?"

"Wrong again!"

"Okay, I give up. Where are we going?"

"Do you remember our last adventure?"

"Yes. We went to see Jacob play a mean trick on his dad and brother."

"Correct! Now we are going to go back and see one of the adventures that Jacob had while he was on his way back home."

✶ ✶ ✶ ✶

"It's dark out. How come it's suddenly so dark out?" I asked.

"Because it's night time," answered Andy.

"Okay. Now my eyes are adjusting to the dark. Is that Jacob crossing that river?"

"Yes. And he has his whole family with him."

We watched as Jacob told his family to go on without him. He said he needed to stay there for a while.

Then, out of the darkness came someone that looked like a man. And the man approached Jacob.

Suddenly Jacob and this stranger began to wrestle.

On and on the wrestling match went. And it looked like Jacob was winning.

"Who is that person that Jacob is fighting?" I asked Andy.

"You wouldn't believe me if I told you," Andy answered.

"Is it an angel? Is it some kind of spirit being?"

"It's about time for the sun to come up. Why don't we just watch and see what happens?"

Then just as easy as could be, the stranger reached out and simply touched Jacob's hip, and immediately Jacob's hip went out of place.

Jacob screamed out in pain. But even with his hip out of place, and with his face winching in pain, Jacob refused to let go.

"It's almost daybreak. Let me go!" said the stranger.

"I have you in my best head lock and I am not going to let go unless you bless me!" replied Jacob.

"Okay. What is your name?" asked the stranger.

"My name is Jacob."

"Your name will no longer be called Jacob. From now on you will be called Israel, because you have struggled with God and with men, and have overcome."

Then Jacob asked, "Since I have won the wrestling match tell me your name."

"Why do you ask my name?"

Then, instead of telling Jacob his name, the stranger blessed him again.

"Wow" I shouted! "Did Jacob just wrestle with who I think that was?"

"Who do you think it was?"

"God!"

"Well, apparently that is also who Jacob thought it was, because he named the place where they wrestled *Peniel*. He said he named it that because that is where he saw God face to face and yet his life was spared."

The thought of someone actually wrestling with God must have shaken me so much that it woke me up.

Wrestling with God! That was all I could think as I lay there in my bed. Wrestling with God!

"Did Jacob actually beat God in a wrestling match?" I asked myself. "There was no way a mere man could out wrestle God!"

And then it hit me! "Who is God?" I asked myself.

And then I answered myself, "Our Father in heaven!"

Then I remembered the times that my dad let me *win* when we wrestled. *Yes. God could have knocked more than Jacob's hip out with a single touch.* He could have knocked every *joint in his body out of whack!*

But how cool is that Almighty God cared for Jacob so much that He took time to leave heaven, and take on the form of a man, and wrestle with Jacob… just so He could bless him!

And then I had a really neat thought. From now on every time I sneeze and someone says *bless you*, I am going to remember this story of God blessing Jacob and giving him a new name!

The last image in my mind as I went back to sleep was of me in my wrestling outfit.

Bright flames and *MM* were on my chest. And of course Andy was there with *AA* on his chest.

Then I saw God come charging onto the scene. He was dressed in white with *GG* on His chest.

The *GG* stood for *GREAT GOD*!

Discuss the following questions with your parents or a friend:

- How long did Jacob wrestle with the "stranger"?
- What part of Jacob's body was injured as they wrestled?
- What new name was Jacob given?

CHAPTER 9: A DREAM ABOUT A DREAMER

Hey Dad" I asked. "Do dreams have meanings?"

"Why do you ask?" replied my dad.

"I have been having some really interesting dreams lately!"

"Well" said my dad, "According to the Bible dreams can have a special meaning. However, most dreams relate to what we have done or seen during the day. The thoughts that are on our mind when we go to sleep are then what we dream about."

"Grandpa says he has bad dreams after he eats too much pepperoni pizza," I said.

With a grin, my dad replied, "There may be some truth to that!"

And wouldn't you know it, it actually happened just that way. We had pepperoni pizza for supper that night.

So I had dreaming on my mind when I drifted off to sleep.

The next thing I knew I was having the greatest dream ever!

I was dreaming that I could fly! I was swooping in and out of clouds! I was spinning and flying upside down… and sideways!

One moment I would be traveling at supersonic speed, and the next moment I was flying in slow motion.

And then in my dream I was flying so high that I was above all of the clouds and I could see every star in the sky. All of the lights on the earth looked like little pin points. And then out of nowhere… wouldn't you know it… Andy shows up!

"Hey Matthew!" shouted Andy. "Look at you. You are flying! You don't need me for this next adventure; you can fly there all on your own!"

"Maybe I don't *need* you, but I sure would like it if you'd come with me anyway!"

"Not a problem," replied Andy. "I'm not doing anything anyway. What would you like to do?"

"Believe it or not, I'd like to lie down and take a nap."

"Wait just a second. You are in one of your dreams, and at the same time you are dreaming of taking a nap?"

"Yes," I replied.

Then in my dream, I started taking a nap.

And then guess what happened???

In my dream of me taking a nap, I started having a dream! Isn't that crazy?

Within my dream I was having another dream!

And then in my dream within my dream... guess who showed up again?

Andy! Andy showed up again!

"This is starting to get confusing," said Andy. "Why don't we just pick up where we were in the other dream where you could fly?"

"Sounds good to me," I said.

"Since you are dreaming about dreaming, why don't we go back in time and see one of the most famous dreamers in the Bible?"

"I bet I know who you are talking about" I said. "I bet you are talking about *Joseph the Dreamer*."

"You are correct!"

"Do you know who Joseph's dad was?" asked Andy as we began to soar through the clouds.

"I think his dad was Jacob, the famous wrestler in the Bible that we watched as he wrestled with God."

"Correct again!" said Andy.

As we were flying, Andy gave me a little background on Joseph.

He told me how that Joseph was the favorite son of Jacob because he was born when Jacob was very old. In fact, Andy said that Jacob loved Joseph so much he had a special coat made for him that became known as the *coat of many colors*.

When his brothers saw that Joseph was the favorite son, and the special coat, it made them very jealous.

"And then Joseph had a dream," said Andy. "And it all started when he was just 17 years old."

"Wait a second" I said. "Let me see if I have this right. Now I am dreaming about some else that had a dream in the middle of my dream?"

Andy grinned real big. "That must have been an extra-large pepperoni pizza you ate last night!" he said with laugh.

Andy continued, "In Joseph's dream he was binding sheaves of grain with all of his brothers. And suddenly all of the sheaves of his brothers bowed down to Joseph's sheave."

"I bet they didn't like that," I said.

"You would win that bet!" Andy replied, "His brothers starting yelling at him. And according to the Bible, it says they actually started hating him!"

Andy continued, "After seeing his brothers get mad about the first dream, you would think he would have known better than to tell his brothers his next dream!"

"What was his next dream?" I asked.

"In his next dream he dreamed that the sun and moon and stars were bowing down to him."

"Oh, that could not have ended well!"

Andy scrunched up his face until most of his freckles disappeared. "No, it did not end well. His brothers got so mad they decided to take his precious coat from him and kill him!"

"Kill him?"

"Yes. They decided to kill him!"

By then Andy and I had arrived at a place that appeared to be out in the middle of nowhere.

"Look over there. That is Joseph's brothers. They are out tending sheep and they see him coming. Let's get closer so you can hear what happens."

We crept closer and hid behind some nearby bushes.

"Look who is coming! It's the *Dreamer*," one of the brothers said sarcastically.

"I've got an idea," said one of the other brothers. "There is no one out here to see what we are doing. Why don't we kill him and throw him in that pit in the ground?"

"That's a great idea," another one of the brothers said. "We can say a ferocious animal ate him!"

Rueben did not like how the conversation was going, so he spoke up and said, "Let's not kill him. Let's just throw him in that pit."

Just then Joseph came up over the last little hill and his brothers ran out to meet him.

They quickly knocked him to the ground, and stripped his coat from him. Then they threw him in the big pit in the ground.

I could tell that they were debating what to do next.

Poor Joseph! He could not believe what was happening to him. How could his own brothers do this horrible thing to him?

As I watched it reminded me of some of the mean things I did to my little sister. I love aggravating her. But I could not imagine doing something this bad!

Joseph was now crying. "What are you guys doing?" he cried up from the pit. "I'm going to tell dad when I get back home!"

His brothers ignored his cries, and actually sat down and started eating their lunch.

These brothers are the worst men I have ever met in my life, I thought. *They have to be the most cold-hearted, and ruthless men around. How could they do something this bad to their little brother?*

"Come on guys. This has gone on long enough" Joseph cried out. "I promise not to bug you with any more of my dreams. Please... please... just let me out... okay? I promise that I won't tell dad what you have done."

"I don't know about you guys, but we can't let him go back home now," said Judah. "If he tells dad what we have done, dad will cut us all out of our inheritance!"

Just then the brothers saw a caravan of travelers coming their way.

Judah spoke up and said, "Instead of killing him, why don't we sell him to these travelers?"

All of the brothers agreed.

So two of them walked over to the pit and threw down a rope, and pulled Joseph up out of the pit.

At first Joseph was completely overjoyed!

"Thanks guys! I knew you wouldn't leave me in that pit! But that sure was a mean prank you just pulled on me!"

"Wait a second… what are you doing? Why are you taking money from these strangers?"

Suddenly it dawned on Joseph just what his brothers were going to do with him. Now his worry turned to pure panic!

"Wait! Wait! Come on guys! Please don't do this! Please! Please!"

But the brothers turned their backs on Joseph and walked away.

After paying the brothers twenty shekels of silver, the travelers quickly tied Joseph's hands together and then hitched the rope to one of their camels.

Off in the direction of Egypt they went, dragging Joseph behind them.

I could not believe the pitiful look on the face of Joseph. His hands, arms, and face were covered with dirt from the pit. Tears were streaming down his face, leaving long dark streaks in the dirt that was on his face! My heart was breaking!

I could tell that Joseph was torn between two emotions; heartbreak and fear.

First he could not believe his own brothers hated him this much.

And second, although he did not know where these travelers were going to take him, he knew that he was going to end up far, far, away from home, in a foreign land.

Poor Joseph!

In my dream I began to cry. How could these brothers be so cruel? How could they sell their little brother to a bunch of strange men, knowing that they would never see him again? I was completely speechless!

As the caravan of travelers disappeared over the distant hill, dragging Joseph behind them, one of the brothers picked up Joseph's coat of many colors.

"What do we want to do with this?"

"Well, we can't take it back home, or dad will figure out we know what happened to Joseph."

"I know," said one of the brothers, "let's kill a goat, and smear its blood all over the coat. Then we can give it to dad and tell him a wild animal killed him."

"That's a great idea! We'll tell him that this is proof that a wild animal killed Joseph."

I turned to Andy. In a quiet, trembling voice I said, "I'm ready to go back home."

The flight back home was very quiet. Andy could tell that I was not in the mood to talk about anything we had just witnessed.

As we flew back I thought about Joseph's elderly father. I could only imagine the heartbreak Jacob suffered when the brothers presented the bloody coat to him.

Then I thought of how scared Joseph must have been, being betrayed by his own flesh and blood, and then sold like a common slave.

Once again I remembered a line from a message our pastor had preached. He said the Bible says that we "reap what we sow," meaning if we do bad things to other people, bad things will happen to us.

Then I remembered on our previous adventure, how Jacob had hurt and deceived his father, Isaac, when he pretended to be Esau. And now the same thing was happening to Jacob. He was being deceived and hurt the same way he deceived his father!

I woke up from my dream.

I guess it is true. I guess you do reap what you sow! Jacob sowed deceit, and he was now reaping deceit. How painful it must have been!

With tears stains on my face I finally drifted back to sleep, but not before wondering what Joseph's brothers were going to reap from treating Joseph so badly? Surely God was not going to let them get away with this!

And I made myself one last sleepy promise. I decided I was going to treat my little sister better! And I was going to try to listen to mom and dad better! And I was going to be more respectful to Mrs. Underwood, my teacher!

Discuss the following questions with your parents or a friend:

- How old was Joseph when he dreamed his brothers would bow to him?
- What special gift did Jacob give to Joseph?
- Where did Joseph's brothers put him?
- How did they decide to get rid of him?

CHAPTER 10: THE ADVENTURES OF THE DREAMER

Several nights went by before Andy stopped by for another adventure. By that time I was getting very anxious to find out exactly what ended up happening to Joseph. I think that is what's known as cliff-hanger. I could hardly wait to find out what happened next!

The last time I saw Joseph he was being dragged behind a camel to a foreign land by a bunch of strange men.

So by the time Andy finally showed up, I was a little bit angry with him.

"Where have you been?" I shouted as he come gliding into my dream.

"Well that sure is a fine how do you do!" he responded. "I don't even get a hello?"

"I'm sorry, but I haven't had a good night's sleep since our last adventure. I have been very curious about Joseph," I said.

"All you had to do was start reading the thirty-ninth chapter of Genesis. That would tell you what happened next," replied Andy.

"I know, but it's much more fun when I get to *see* it!"

"Well, you don't have to worry about Joseph. His faith in God is strong!"

"It had better be! Because I'm sure his faith in his brothers is completely gone!"

"I know," said Andy. "Wasn't that about the hardest thing you have ever had to witness?"

"That's why I have been so anxious to get back and see what happens next!" I shouted.

"Okay. Okay. Just chill out. We can leave right now!"

I didn't want to admit it to Andy, but I was also a little excited about now being able to fly in my dreams. I could hardly wait for us to lift off!

As we went zooming off into the darkness, I shouted out at Andy, "I'm getting pretty good at this flying thing. So you had better stay close to my tail or you are going to get left behind!"

"So after just one night of flying on your own you think you are now an expert, huh?"

"Watch this!" I exclaimed. And I took off just as fast as I could possibly fly.

You are never going to believe what Andy did! He passed me!

But he didn't just fly past me… he flew past me flying backwards!

And not only was he flying backwards, he was also pretending to do the backstroke like he was swimming!

"Show off!" I shouted as we laughed together.

Have you ever heard the expression *don't get your tail feathers ruffled*?

I have heard Grandpa say that to Grandma when she starts getting excited over some dumb thing he had done.

Well, now I was actually getting to see someone with their feathers ruffled!

Andy looked extremely funny as he was flying backwards. With his feathers sticking straight up, he reminded me of a cockatoo!

I was laughing so hard, it was all I could do to stay air borne!

"Okay. I give up. You win!" I shouted above the whistling sound that was coming from Andy's ruffled wings!

Andy did a loopty loop and then glided in next to me in formation, finally flying frontwards again.

I could never stay angry at Andy for very long!

"Have you ever been on a roller coaster?" asked Andy, changing the subject.

"I sure have," I replied.

"You know how you are up one minute and then down the next?"

"That's what makes it so fun," I responded.

"Well, just to give you a heads up, that is how Joseph's life turns out over the next several years," Andy stated.

Just then we began flying over the outskirts of a large city.

"Where are we?" I asked.

"Egypt. Do you see that great big mansion over there?"

"Yes. Who lives there? They must really have a lot of money!"

"A man named Potiphar lives there and he is a captain in the Egyptian army."

"He sure does have a very nice home. Wow, just look at all of the beautiful landscaping around his home. It looks like he is very wealthy," I said.

"That's because he is," Andy replied.

Andy continued, "Now look down there on that balcony. Who does that look like?"

"It looks like Joseph!"

"Yep, it sure is!"

"What is he doing in that big beautiful mansion?" I asked.

"He works there. Actually, he is now in charge of everything that goes on at the mansion."

"Wow, he has really done well for himself, hasn't he?"

"Do you remember how I told you that his faith in God is strong?" Andy asked.

"Yes."

"Well, this is proof of that. God has not only blessed Joseph but God has also blessed Potiphar because of Joseph."

Andy continued, "Joseph was sold to Potiphar by those travelers, and almost immediately God gave favor to Joseph. And by God giving Joseph favor, Potiphar was also granted favor. Joseph started out working as a servant, but very quickly was promoted to being in charge of all of Potiphar's estate."

"You mean that Potiphar was blessed just because Joseph worked for him?"

"Absolutely!"

"So I will be blessed just by hanging around with the right people?" I asked.

"Sure enough!" Andy advised. "So keep that in mind when you choose your friends."

"Well, if Joseph's life is like a roller coaster he sure is a high point right now."

"See that beautiful woman walking up behind Joseph on the balcony?" Andy asked.

"Who is she?" I asked back in response.

"She is Potiphar's wife. And she is not a nice lady."

"What is she doing?"

"She is trying to get Joseph to kiss her."

"Well that ain't right!" I exclaimed. "If she is married to Potiphar, the only man she should be kissing is her husband!"

"Right you are." said Andy.

"Look," I said to Andy, "Joseph is pushing her away. But she sure looks angry."

As we watched I asked, "Why is she shouting at him?"

"Because she is a spoiled little rich lady that is used to getting everything she wants." Andy responded.

"Well she sure isn't very happy right now."

Then I saw Potiphar walking up to the front of their mansion. Immediately his wife went running out to him shouting out that Joseph had attacked her!

"She's lying! Come on Andy, we have to go tell Potiphar the truth!"

"Oh no," I continued. "Potiphar really looks mad!"

We watched as Potiphar called for some guards to come and arrest Joseph. Then they dragged him away. And the whole time Joseph was screaming out, "I am innocent! I am innocent!"

"Where are they taking him?"

"To prison," Andy replied.

"But it's her word against his. That isn't fair."

"Listen to me Matthew," Andy said. "You might as well learn right now that life is not always fair!"

"But Joseph is such a good young man. Surely God will swoop down and rescue him this time. He's already been through enough with what his brothers did to him."

"Yes. You are right. He is a good man. But sometimes bad things happen to good people."

"Yeah, I know you are right. There's a really nice man that goes to our church that has been sick a long time. I asked Dad why he was so sick, and he said that even when life is bad, God is still good."

"Your dad is absolutely correct," Andy replied.

"So what's going to happen to Joseph now?" I asked.

Then Andy told me the story of how Joseph was thrown into prison.

But the same way Joseph found favor with Potiphar and was elevated to a higher position in Potiphar's house, he also found favor with the officials that were in charge of the prison, and was elevated to a higher position while he was in prison.

"But what about his dreams?"

"Dreams were still a very important part of Joseph's life, even though he was in prison," Andy replied.

Andy continued on by telling me about two prisoners that had dreams. And Joseph was able to tell them the meanings of their dreams.

He told the butler for the king that he would be released from prison in 3 days. But he told the baker that he would be killed in three days.

And it happened exactly the way Joseph said it would. As the butler was being released Joseph shouted out to him, "Remember what I did for you when you go before the king."

"I will." replied the butler.

"Did the butler do what he promised?" I asked.

"Not at first."

"How long before the butler remembered to help Joseph?"

"Two years."

"Two years!"

I paused in my talk with Andy and thought about what he had just told me.

At my age I could not imagine having to wait two years for anything. I have a hard time waiting for two minutes!

"So how long was Joseph in prison?" I asked.

"He was seventeen years old when he was sold by his brothers, and he was thirty years old when he was released from prison. What is thirty minus seventeen?"

"Thirteen," I said. "He was in prison for thirteen years?"

"The Bible doesn't give us the exact number, but he was in prison for a long time."

"So how did he finally get out of prison? Did he dig a tunnel?"

"No."

"Did he saw through the prison bars?"

"No."

"Did he disguise how he looked and trick the guards into letting him out?"

"No. Just be quiet and I'll tell you. The butler that was released from prison went to work for Pharaoh the king. One night the king had a dream and when he woke up he was very troubled by the dream."

"What was his dream?" I asked.

"Well, that was the problem. He was very troubled by the dream but he couldn't remember what the dream was about."

"I sure don't have that problem. I seem to be able to remember my dreams in full detail," I responded.

"That's because of me!" Andy stated.

"That is true. You help make my dreams very memorable! So what happened next?"

"The king called in all his wise men and magicians to see if they could tell him about his dream. But none of them could do so."

"Wow! This is really cool. I bet that was when the butler remembered that Joseph had told him the meaning of his dream!"

"Exactly!"

Andy proceeded to tell me how the butler told the king that Joseph could interpret dreams. So the king sent for him.

"What did the dream mean?"

"Oh Joseph didn't just tell him what the dream meant. First he told exactly what he had dreamed."

"Wait a second. Without anyone telling him about the dream in advance, Joseph knew what the king had dreamed about?" I shouted.

"Yep!"

"I bet that blew the kings mind!"

"Well, it sure let the king know that Joseph was the real deal. I mean if he was able tell the king exactly what he dreamed about, surely the king would believe him when he told him what the dreams meant."

I had to stop and think again.

"Was Joseph like those advertisements on late night TV where those weird people claim to be able to read your mind?" I asked.

"No, you goof ball!" Andy replied. "Those people are fakes. They are just good at reading how people act and think. Then they use that information to make it look like they are mind readers."

"So Joseph didn't wear a turban on his head or have a crystal ball?"

"No."

"Did he roll his eyes back in his head and start making weird noises?"

"NO! Quit asking me such goofy questions."

I was tempted to keep asking questions just to aggravate Andy, but decided to move on.

"So what was the meaning of the king's dream?" I asked.

"God revealed to Joseph that there were going to be seven years when the crops would grow very well. During those years the land of Egypt would have plenty of food. And then there would be seven years of famine. During those years the fields would not produce any crops."

"And the king believed him?"

"Yep!"

"Then what happened?" I asked.

"Joseph told the king that he should set aside food during the seven years of plenty so that they would have food to eat during the seven years of drought."

"Did the king listen?"

"Not only did he listen but he put Joseph in charge of the whole program!"

"No way!" I shouted.

"He sure did. In fact the king gave Joseph so much power that he was like the vice president of the whole country of Egypt!"

Now I really had to stop and think about this whole story.

After being betrayed and sold by his brothers...

After being falsely accused by Potiphar's wife...

After years and years in prison for a crime he did not commit...

After telling the meaning of the butler's dream and the butler being released from prison, only to forget to help…

After waiting two more years after the butler was released for him to finally remember to help Joseph…

After all of that… Joseph is not only released from prison, but in the matter of just a few hours he goes from being a prisoner to being the vice president of Egypt!

"Our God is an *awesome* God, isn't He?" I shouted out to Andy.

"Oh Matthew, if you only knew!"

"What does that mean?"

"As an angel I have lived with God for a long, long time. And what you have just witnessed in this dream is a drop in the bucket compared to just how great, majestic, and totally awesome God is!"

"I don't think there is room in my head for any more information! This is mind blowing!" I exclaimed to Andy.

For some reason Andy found that statement to be extremely funny. I think he was imagining my head exploding.

At first he giggled. Then he laughed. Then he grabbed his side and started laughing so hard he sounded like a donkey heehawing! The red curly strands of his hair were flopping down over his face. And his face turned so red that all of his freckles disappeared! And his short little wings were just quivering back and forth!

Then I began to laugh at Andy.

And laugh. And laugh. And laugh.

"Are you ready to head back home?" he asked as he wiped the tears of laughter from his cheeks.

"I reckon so."

Off we went flying back home and laughing all the way.

Have you ever seen two birds playing and chasing each other?

That is exactly how Andy and I looked. Up and down I chased after him. Around and around he chased me back, as we flew into the clouds.

Then I was awake. But not just awake… awake because I was laughing out loud in my sleep.

Tears were streaming down my cheek. But this time it was tears of laughter on my face… not like the tears of pain I felt for Joseph on the previous adventure.

Andy was right, I thought, *that adventure sure was like riding a roller coaster!*

I lay there in my bed and stretched out both arms high above my head, pretending I was on a roller coaster. I could almost feel my stomach lifting and dropping.

Then I remembered reading in the book of Psalms that we should lift our hands in praise to God. So I just kept both of my hands in the air and I prayed this prayer…

Dear Lord, I am so thankful that You sent Andy to help me understand who You are so much better. Thank You for being such a great God to Joseph. Thank you for letting me know that when I grow up to be a man and I find myself in a bad situation, I can still know that You have not forgotten about me, the same way You never forgot about Joseph. I know that You watch out for me every day. But as much as I thank You for sending Andy to me, I want to say thank You even more for sending Jesus Your Son to die for me and take away my sins! Amen.

Discuss the following questions with your parents or a friend:

- What was the man's name that put Joseph in charge of his property?
- Who were the two men in prison with Joseph?
- What happened to the two men?
- How did Joseph end up being released from prison?
- What position did Joseph receive after he told the King about his dream?

CHAPTER 11: DREAMS DO COME TRUE

"A re you ready to see what happens to Joseph next?" Andy asked, as he flew into my dream.

"Sure thing," I responded. "I really liked how the last dream ended. And I can't wait to see what happens next."

"Have you ever had someone tell you *I told you so?*"

"Yes. Kevin, the smartest kid in my class, is like that! He is constantly telling the rest of us things that he thinks we don't know. And when something turns out the way he said it would, he always smirks and says *I told you so.*"

"I don't know if Joseph ever said *I told you so*, but he sure could have." Andy said.

"So the dreams he had about his brothers did come true?" I asked.

"Yep!"

"His brothers actually bowed down to him?"

"Yep!"

"Well let's get going. I don't want to miss seeing those mean brothers bowing down before their little brother!"

As we glided into the outskirts of Egypt Andy said, "Look over there at that caravan of travelers."

79

"What about them?" I asked.

"Guess who they are?"

"Apparently they are related to Joseph's story, so I am going guess that they are Joseph's brothers."

"Yep, they sure are," said Andy.

"They look very worried."

"They are," said Andy. "They are coming to Egypt because Egypt is the only place that has any food. If they don't get food to take back home, their families are going to starve to death."

"And they have no idea that Joseph is the vice president of Egypt?" I asked.

"They don't have a clue."

Then Andy told me how Joseph's brothers had to go see Joseph, because he was the one in charge of all of the food.

Then Andy said, "Guess what the brothers do when they're brought before Joseph?"

I could see a gleam in Andy's eyes, so I knew the answer was going to be good.

"What?" I asked in anticipation.

"When the brothers were brought into Joseph's office… *they bowed down before him!*"

When he told me that I started jumping up and down!

"It happened just like Joseph said it would in his dream!" I shouted.

"Yep!"

"Now I get it. Now I know why you brought up the *I-told-you-so* comment earlier!" I exclaimed.

Continuing on, excitedly I asked, "So did Joseph tell them? Did he tell them who he was? And then did he say… *na-na-na-na-na* … I told you so!"

"No," said Andy.

"Well why not? I sure would have! So what did he do?"

Then Andy told me how Joseph recognized his brothers. But, they did not recognize him.

He said, remembering the dreams that he had as a boy, Joseph decided to play a little game with them.

"What kind of game?" I asked.

"He started out by accusing them of being spies."

"Oh yeah! I love it! I bet that scared them silly!" I said.

Andy then told me how they tried to explain to Joseph their situation. They explained to Joseph how they were all brothers. How their father sent them to Egypt to buy food. And then they said something that instantly got Joseph's attention. *They told Joseph that they left their youngest brother at home with their father.*

"So how did Joseph react when they mentioned the youngest brother?" I asked.

"He told the brothers he still thought they were spies. And he was going to put all of them, except one, in prison. The one brother he did not put in prison must go back home and bring the youngest brother back to Egypt to prove that they were not spies."

"Oh wow!" I shouted. "He decided to put them in prison so that they could get a little taste of what he went through when he was put in prison!"

"Yep. He sure did."

"Then what happened?"

"He acted like he changed his mind and he put *all of them* in prison!"

"For how long?"

"For three days."

"Oh this is really a cool story." I said. "Do you think he peeked around the corner of the prison to see how they were handling being in jail?"

"I'm sure he did."

"Then what happened?" I asked.

"He told them that he had changed his mind again. He told them he would only keep one of them in Egypt while the rest went back home to deliver food to their families. But the others must bring back their youngest brother."

"Guess what the brothers said when Joseph told them the revised plan?" Andy asked.

"What?" I asked.

"They said they were having all these problems because of what they had done to their brother, meaning Joseph!"

"No way. They actually made that confession?"

"They sure did," replied Andy.

"So even after all those years they never forgot about what they did to Joseph?"

"No. Apparently what they did to Joseph haunted them all those years."

"And they didn't realize that when they were talking about what they did to Joseph, he was standing right there in front of them?"

"Right again," said Andy.

Maybe they weren't as bad as I thought… if it bothered them that much… I pondered to myself.

Then I asked Andy, "So Joseph is standing right there the whole time they are talking about him?"

"Yes. And get this… Joseph spoke the Egyptian language and used an interpreter when he spoke to them."

"How come?"

"He didn't want them to know who he was yet."

"So when the brothers were speaking to each other in their Hebrew language, they had no idea he could understand everything they said?" I asked.

"Yep!"

"Oh this just gets better and better!" I shouted. "What happened next?"

"Let's move closer so you can see for yourself how Joseph reacts," he said.

I could not believe my eyes. Joseph had turned away from his brothers and was crying!

"Why is he crying?" I asked.

"Well, think about it. He hasn't seen his brothers for a long, long time. I'm sure he still had a lot of good memories about his childhood."

Then I couldn't believe what Joseph did next. He quickly dried his tears and commanded the guards to take Simeon, the youngest brother, and tie his hands together and take him away!

Then, continuing to speak in Egyptian so the brothers wouldn't understand him, Joseph told the guards to put the silver the brothers used to pay for their grain back in the bags with the food they had purchased.

"Now what is he doing?" I asked Andy. "It looks like he is just messing with them!"

"He sure is!" said Andy.

We watched as the brothers loaded up their donkeys and headed back home.

"Do you want to stay here and watch Joseph and see if he decides to mess with Simeon? Or do you want to follow the other brothers and see how they react when they find the silver in their grain sacks?" asked Andy.

I had to think about this one for a minute. "I want to follow the brothers. How long does it take before they find the silver?" I asked.

"Not long," replied Andy.

Andy and I floated above the brothers as they began the long journey back home. They were very quiet. I could tell that they were deep in thought. I'm sure they were regretting what they had done to Joseph those many years ago.

"It's time to stop for the night," one of the brothers said.

One brother started setting up a tent for them to sleep in. One started gathering wood for a fire. Another brother got ready to feed the donkeys.

"Oh no!" another brother shouted. "Oh my goodness. We are doomed. God must have completely forsaken us. Surely God has turned His back on us!"

Hearing the outburst, the other brothers quickly dropped what they were doing and rushed to where he was standing. He had his grain sack in his hand and a look of pure panic on his face.

"What's wrong?"

"Look! Look here in my sack. The silver I gave the vice president to pay for our grain is back here in my sack!"

The brothers looked at one another in disbelief.

"What should we do?"

I turned to look at Andy. I was starting to feel torn. On one hand I wanted to see the brothers punished for what they had done to Joseph. But on the other hand I could see how sincerely dismayed they were.

That night we watched as the brothers tossed and turned in their sleep. I don't know what they were dreaming about, but obviously they were having nightmares because of what was happening to them. I'm sure they were dreaming about the *dreamer*.

During the following days of their journey they remained silent. And at night, even though they were exhausted, they did not find rest in their sleep.

After several days of travel, they finally reached home.

Jacob was anxiously waiting for their return to find out if they were able to get food.

"Yes, we have grain. But the trip did not end well," they told their elderly father. The Egyptian (speaking of Joseph) of the land treated us like we were criminals. He accused of being spies. And worst of all he refused to let Simeon come back home with us."

"What did he do with Simeon?" Jacob asked.

"He had him tied up and thrown in prison!"

Their elderly father sank to his knees. "What do we do now?" he cried out, as tears began rolling down his face.

"Not only that. The Egyptian said we have to bring Benjamin, our youngest brother, back to Egypt if we wish to prove we are not spies. If we do so he promised to let Simeon come back home with us."

"Oh my! What have we done?" exclaimed Jacob.

I could see pure torment on the face of the old man.

Then the brothers began emptying their grain sacks. To their alarm in every sack was the bag of silver they had given to Joseph in payment for the grain!

I had never seen that amount of pure terror on anyone's face. The brothers were so distraught they did not know what to do next.

And poor Jacob… I thought their old father was going to die on the spot.

Trembling and shaking, Jacob began shouting out to his sons, "Joseph is gone… Simeon is gone… And now you want to take my youngest son, Benjamin, back to Egypt? Everything and everyone is against me!"

Reuben walked over to his father and knelt down beside him. "I give you my word, Father. If we do not bring Simeon and Benjamin back with us you may put both of my sons to death."

I looked at Andy in disbelief of what I had just heard! Andy looked at me, shaking his head back and forth.

This had now gone to a completely different level. This was really getting crazy now.

"No!" shouted Jacob. "I will never let Benjamin go down to Egypt! Joseph is dead, and Benjamin is the only young son I have left! If anything should happen to him I would surely die!"

Again, as can only happen in a dream, Andy and I watched as time jumped forward.

Jacob and the brothers had used up all of the grain they had brought from Egypt.

Sitting around the table the brothers finally got up enough nerve to approach their father about going back to Egypt to get more food. Realizing that they had no other choice, Jacob finally gave in. Reluctantly he agreed that they should go. And even more reluctantly, he let Benjamin go also.

"But here is what you will do," said Jacob. "Take as many spices, nuts, and honey as we can spare with you, along with twice the amount of silver you took last time. And may Almighty God be with you and give you mercy so that Simeon and Benjamin may come back home safely with you."

I felt so very sorry for Jacob as I saw the unbearable amount of pain the old man was suffering. And just when I thought I had heard it all, Jacob began to rock back and forth. Back and forth… back and forth he rocked, as he sat there in the dust, mumbling over and over, "I am so sad… I am so very sad."

Long gone were any feelings I had of wanting to see the brothers suffer any more.

"Can we just skip ahead to where they meet with Joseph?" I asked Andy.

"Sure," he responded.

Time Jump.

Joseph was watching anxiously as his brothers came slowly down the road.

When he saw that Benjamin was with them he turned to one of the servants and quickly told him to go prepare a meal.

Then he told another servant to inform his brothers that he wanted them to eat lunch with him.

"This is going to be so cool," I told Andy. "This is going to be the best family reunion ever!"

But as the brothers were being taken to Joseph's house they began whispering to each other… *What is this Egyptian up to now? Do you think he knows about the silver that was put back in our sacks? Is he going to throw us back in prison? What if he makes us his slaves?*

"Wow," I said to Andy. "Joseph has these guys completely running in circles."

One of the brothers approached Joseph's servant and told him, "Please, sir, we came here the first time to buy food. But somehow the silver we used to buy the food ended up back in our sacks. We have brought double the amount this time. Please be merciful to us!"

Then the brothers received the first ray of hope since this whole trip started so long ago.

"It's all right," said the servant. "Don't be afraid. Your God, the God of your father, has given you plenty of treasure in your sacks. I have received all the silver I need!"

For the first time I saw a few small smiles on the brother's faces.

Then I thought they were all going to start dancing when the servant brought Simeon out to them. They began jumping up and down just like our fifth grade basketball team did when they won the Christmas Basketball Tournament!

When Joseph came out to meet them I watched as they bowed down and presented him with the gifts of spices and nuts they brought to give him.

"Look," I whispered loudly to Andy. "They are bowing before Joseph again… just like Joseph dreamed they would!"

"How is everyone doing?" Joseph asked through the interpreter. And they all responded that they were doing well.

"How is your aged father that you told me about? Is he still alive?"

"Yes, our father is alive and doing well."

And again the brothers bowed as low to the ground as they could. They had now bowed before Joseph *three times!*

I thought… *If they bow any lower they will have their faces in the dirt!*

Looking at Benjamin, Joseph asked, "Is this the youngest brother you told me about?"

"Yes."

"May God be gracious to you, my son," Joseph said to Benjamin.

Then I saw big tears welling up in Joseph's eyes.

Quickly Joseph turned and left to find a private place to weep. When he finally got control of his emotions, he washed his face and returned to where the brothers were seated.

"Go ahead and serve everyone," Joseph said to his servants, still speaking Egyptian so that his brothers did not know who he was.

But Joseph did not sit and eat with his brothers. He ate by himself.

Apparently Joseph could not resist messing with his brothers one last time. This time he told the servants to seat the brothers in order, from the oldest to the youngest.

Once they were seated the brothers quickly noticed that they were seated from the oldest to the youngest.

"How did they know to seat us in order according to how old we are? What is going on here," they whispered to each other.

They were completely astonished!

"Look at their faces," I said to Andy, with a big grin on my face. "There Joseph goes again… acting like a typical brother! Surely he's going to tell them who he is now, right?"

Andy just grinned at me with that silly crooked grin.

"No way! He is *still* not done messing with them?"

"Nope!" replied Andy.

"Now what does he have up his sleeve?"

Joseph rose from eating and went to one of his servants and started whispering to him.

Andy and I moved in close so we could hear.

"Okay. Here is what I want you to do this time," Joseph was whispering to the servant. "Put their silver back in the sacks. Only this time put it right on top so that it is the first thing they see!"

"Oh no! Here he goes again," I said to Andy.

We both began giggling like a couple of little girls!

But Joseph still wasn't done.

"And… Take my special silver cup and put it in Benjamin's sack, along with the silver he used to buy grain."

"They are going to flip out!" I shouted to Andy. "They… are… going… to… go… crazy!"

"Okay. Let's fast forward again," I anxiously said to Andy.

Time Jump to the next morning.

✮ ✮ ✮ ✮

The next morning the brothers were sent on their way back home.

But just as they reached the edge of the city limits Joseph sent several servants to catch them.

When the servants caught up with them they shouted, "Are you guys idiots! Why have you been so evil when you were just treated so well?

"Someone has stolen our master's silver cup. So we need everyone to open up your sacks so we can search them. Our master said that whoever stole the cup will become his slave. The rest can return back home!"

Each brother, from the oldest to the youngest, began opening their sacks.

We could hear sighs of relief as one after the other opened their sacks to see that the silver cup was not in their bag.

When it finally came to Benjamin's turn to open his sack I could see the tension on each brother's face. I could see it in their eyes...

Please... please... please... Don't let it be in Benjamin's sack!

Slowly Benjamin untied the knot that held the sack closed.

Slowly he opened the mouth of the sack.

Immediately everyone knew that the cup was in his sack!

Benjamin's eyes darted from brother to brother... he cried out in anguish.

"How?" "How can this be?" "How did this cup end up in my sack?"

"How dare you steal our master's cup," the head servant shouted at Benjamin. "This is a wicked, wicked, thing you have done!"

I have never seen such sheer devastation! All of the brothers were so panic stricken that they began ripping their clothes.

"Why are they doing that?" I asked Andy.

"In those days ripping your clothes was a way of expressing deep sorrow and pain," he answered.

The servants quickly tied Benjamin up and began dragging him back to Joseph's house. The brothers stumbled along behind them, with looks of sheer disbelief on their faces.

"Look at them," said Andy. "I think they are in shock."

"I know. They are walking like they are a bunch of zombies." I said.

That was the only description I could think of to describe what the brothers looked like. It was like they were sleep walking as they stumbled along.

Just like zombies!

As soon as Joseph walked into the room where they were, the brothers threw themselves down on the ground before him. And this time they literally had their faces down in the dirt. *Again...* they were bowing before him!

"What have you done!" shouted Joseph. "Did you really think I would not find out what you have done?"

Judah lifted his tear stained face up from the dirt... "What can we say my lord?" "How can we prove that we are innocent?" "We will all become your slaves... not just Benjamin."

"No. I am a just man. I will only keep the one who stole the cup," Joseph responded. "The rest can return to your father."

Getting down on his hands and knees Judah crawled to the feet of Joseph.

With tears streaming through the dirt that was now on his face... And his voice quivering with remorse, Judah made the most pitiful plea I ever heard. "Please sir... Please master... May I have just a moment of your time? I know that you are a powerful man in Egypt, so please have mercy on us."

"Speak!" said Joseph.

Then, with his voice cracking with emotion, Judah told Joseph about his father and his youngest brother. He told him how their father did not want Benjamin to come to Egypt with them. But their father finally agreed because that was the only way for them to get more food.

Judah continued, "Our father told us that he had already lost one young son that had been killed by wild animals. He said that if we do not bring Benjamin back home with us he will surely die of a broken heart! So, I will take Benjamin's place. I will be your slave for the rest of my life."

"Just please... please... Please let Benjamin return home to my father."

Seeing that Judah was willing to give up his life to save the life of Benjamin, Joseph could no longer contain his emotions.

"Everyone out of here!" he shouted.

When everyone else had left the room, Joseph stood quietly in front of his brothers.

I could see that he was trying to figure out the best way to tell them who he really was.

Leaning forward he looked each brother right in the eyes.

Then he spoke to them.

Only this time he spoke in Hebrew,their native language, so that they could understand him.

"I... am... Joseph!" he whispered loudly.

His brothers looked at him.

Then they looked at each other.

"What!!!!"

This time he shouted as loud as he could... "I.. AM... JOSEPH! I AM YOUR LITTLE BROTHER!!! THE BROTHER YOU SOLD INTO SLAVERY!!!"

Slowly it began to dawn on them.

They looked at Joseph. Then they looked at each other. Then they looked at Joseph again.

This was indeed their little brother! This was the one they put in the pit! This was the one that they sold to the traveling merchants!

And here he is... standing in front of them... Alive!!!

And not only is he alive, he is second in command in the whole land of Egypt!

I turned to Andy and he was crying with joy the same way I was!

I ran toward him and he instinctively knew what I had in mind.

Flying through the air we tried to chest bump each other.

Instead, his belly hit me so hard it knocked both of us to the ground!

We laughed! We cried! We high-fived! And low-fived! And you're-too-slow fived!

"What an awesome end to a story!!!" I shouted to Andy.

"Oh! We're not done yet." He yelled back at me.

"Is my father still alive?" Joseph asked.

"Yes," they replied.

Sensing that his brothers still had doubts about his forgiveness, Joseph said to them "Now, don't be angry with your selves. God had a plan all along. Had you not sold me as a slave I would never have come to Egypt. And had I not come to Egypt our family would have died in the famine."

"What you meant as evil God turned into something good!"

"Now, hurry up and go back home and bring dad back with you!"

"And bring all your wives and kids and grandchildren."

"In fact… just bring whatever you want."

"I will provide everything else that you need!"

Then Joseph ran to his little brother Benjamin and threw his arms around him and began weeping.

Benjamin gave him the biggest bear hug in return and he was crying too!

Then Joseph went from brother to brother, giving each one a kiss as they all wept together!

Time Jump.

✯ ✯ ✯ ✯

"This is one scene I don't want to miss," I said to Andy.

Andy and I had followed the brothers as they went back home to get Jacob.

"Did you notice that they were walking a whole lot faster on this trip home?" I asked Andy.

"Yep!" said Andy.

On the last day of the journey back home the brothers were actually running. They could hardly wait to tell their father the great news!

Running into their father's house they breathlessly shouted in unison, "Joseph is alive!"

Jacob sat there in his rocking chair... stunned! It took several seconds for it to sink in.

"What???" he exclaimed.

They all gathered around Jacob, each one excitedly telling a different part of the story.

"Look!" I said to Andy. "Look at Jacob's face."

We watched as each brother excitedly took terms telling what had happened. With each word the old man's face lit up a little brighter until he was grinning from ear to ear!

"Can it get any better than this?" I asked Andy.

Again Andy just gave me that silly crooked grin.

"What?" I asked.

"Don't you want to see Joseph reunited with his father?" asked Andy.

"Do I!" I shouted.

One More Time Jump.

Andy and I were doing loopity loops... spirals... and all kinds of fancy flying stunts in anticipation of the reunion of Joseph and Jacob.

"Come on... hurry up... I can hardly wait!"

As soon as Joseph received word that his father was near the outskirts of the city he jumped in his chariot that was hooked up to his fastest horses and raced out to meet his father.

We watched as the horses came to a sliding halt. The dust flew up into the air. And before the chariot wheels could stop turning Joseph was already out of the chariot and running to meet his father!

"Dad!" he shouted as he threw his arms around him.

"My son! My son! My son!" Jacob shouted back as he hugged Joseph with every ounce of strength left in his aged body.

"Now I can die in peace," said Jacob as the tears of joy streamed down his face… "Now I can die in peace!"

"Quit grinning." said Andy.

"You quit grinning." I replied.

Andy and I soared high above the clouds on the way back to my bedroom.

"Wow! What an adventure. Thanks Andy. Thanks for showing up in my dreams"

"Hey, it has been great for me as well. But we are just getting started. There are many, many, more Bible adventures in store for us. There are 65 more books of the Bible for us to explore!"

"Really?" I asked.

Andy replied with his favorite word… "Yep!"

Discuss the following questions with your parents or a friend:

- What did Joseph accuse his brothers of being when they first showed up in Egypt?
- What did the brothers find in their sacks of grain?
- What personal belonging of Joseph's did Benjamin find in his sack of grain?
- Joseph told his brothers (fill in the blank): "What you meant as _____ God has turned into _____."

THE END

ACKNOWLEDGEMENTS:

First I want to give thanks to my Lord and Savior Jesus Christ. He has been there beside me every step of my life. To Him be all the glory and honor!

To Jennifer Upchurch, my beautiful, sassy, inspirational wife: You have walked with me these past twenty one years. I love you! The walk has been brighter, happier, and much more adventurous because of you. King Solomon was right. *When I found you I found a good thing and I also found favor from the Lord! (Proverbs 18:22)*

To my children: Heather Roesch, Kyle Upchurch, and Zachary Brandt; to my son-in-law Jason Roesch; and to my hilarious granddaughter, Jaylyn Roesch: All of you have brought me more joy than a man could ever deserve. I am proud of each and every one of you. *I thank God for the many arrows in my quiver! (Psalm 127:3-5)*

In memory of my parents Charles and Mildred Upchurch: Thank you for introducing me to Jesus. Because of you I was able to see that this Bible thing really works. You were the living example of the old song "Little Is Much When God Is In It."

To my siblings: Judy Swindle and husband Bill; Roy Upchurch and wife Kathy; Fay Suarez and husband OJ; Joy Rutherford and husband Bill; and Melody Albanito and husband Fred: Thank you for making growing up so much fun. Also, thank you for not killing me when I was such a pest!

To Jil Rae Curry, my sister-in-law: Thank you for your editing skills!

To the members of The Rock Church, in Centralia, Illinois, were I am so blessed to be allowed to pastor: Your love and support over the last seven years has truly been overwhelming. You are very good sheep! (not baaaad sheep)

To the many wonderful friends that have been there over the years, of which there are too many to mention (other than Gene Gray - my best friend since 4th grade). *A friend loves at all times, and a brother is born for adversity. (Proverbs 17:17)*

To Sarah Mills at *Moments In Photography*: Thank you for the photograph!

In special memory of Mark Shell who went home to be with the Lord on March 27th, 2015: You were my spiritual leader, friend, and pastor. You treated me like a rubber band. You pulled me, pushed me, and stretched me into areas I would have never gone without your encouragement, love, trust, and support. Thank you for the great example you set. Your drive, passion, and vision are a big part of who I am today!

Printed in the United States
By Bookmasters